SHELTERED FROM LOVE

JACQUOLYN MCMURRAY

Book Cover by Get Covers

Edited by Frank Eaton.

A warm mahalo to my critique partners: Laurie Robertson, Joanne Jaytanie, Linda Hornung, and Kristin Wolfgang. Your comments, support, and encouragement are invaluable.

CONTENTS

CHAPTER ONE

GEORGIA STARED AT HER kitchen calendar, arms cinched across her stomach, guilt trapped in her chest. Three long years since William had died. Three years since she'd watched him collapse. Three years since she'd failed to save him.

She drew the morning air into her lungs. Kept to the morning routine William had established when they first moved to their Hawaiian home. Trudging through the garden as she had every morning since his death, Georgia jotted notes in his leather-bound garden journal, recorded the opening of the pink plumeria, and noted the pests that inhabited the plants. She harvested the first ripe grapefruits from the six-year-old citrus tree, cradled one fruit in each hand, and carried them to the kitchen.

Knife poised, she sliced through the thin rind. Juice sprayed into her eyes. Georgia dropped the knife, groped her way to the faucet, and splashed water onto her face. She dried with a kitchen towel and slumped into a kitchen chair. Tears burned her cheeks—the sting no longer from the acidic juice. William should have been there to enjoy the first harvest. And he would have been if only she'd responded more quickly.

Her empty house echoed her sobs until the reverberations settled in her chest and only the familiar hollowness remained. She stared beyond her garden wall; her gaze skittered past the Royal Palms that lined the drive to the crisp line where the sky met the Pacific Ocean. Close by, dogs barked. She stood for a better view. A miniature schnauzer and a toy poodle faced off—both on leashes, both pulling on their leads, both behaving more boldly than their size would suggest. Their humans scooped them up and cuddled them.

Georgia's lips curled into a half smile. It would be lovely to have a pet again. Another living thing to share the empty rooms. But she knew better than to entertain the idea. Her heart craved companionship, but William's objections still haunted her—pets were messy and noisy and didn't belong in the house. Sighing, she glanced at her watch. At least she had her volunteer work at the animal shelter, where the animals provided some short-term relief for her loneliness.

Driving to the shelter, Georgia ran her fingers over the raised letters on the keychain she bought when they were planning their move to Hawai'i. B-e-l-i-e-v-e. She whispered the word. Struggling to embrace the affirmation, she pulled into the parking area and told herself to get a grip.

Inside, she observed another successful adoption. Georgia grinned. One more animal united with a family. She waltzed down the hallway humming "You Are My Sunshine," then paused and shook her head. She hadn't sung that song since Samantha was ten years old—back when their family home radiated warmth and love.

Her hand flew to her trembling chin. Would she ever again have such love in her house? Georgia inhaled a cleansing breath and counted her blessings on the exhale. She was healthy. Samantha visited twice a year. Her volunteer work at the shelter was rewarding, and Lani was the most supportive best friend she'd ever known.

Georgia squared her shoulders and headed for her favorite dog. Onyx was curled up in a corner of his enclosure. "Good morning, fella."

He roused, swished his tail, and pawed the fence. Georgia released the latch and fell to her knees to hug him. She loved working with Rottweilers—had developed a soft spot for them as a teen. Onyx craved attention, and Georgia loved giving it to him. At seven years old, the chances were slim that anyone would adopt him. At least the shelter had a no-kill policy. "Come on, Onyx. Let's play ball."

His head held high, Onyx strutted to the play yard. Georgia ran her fingers through his wiry black hair. He sat on her foot and peered up. She grinned and threw the ball. Onyx wagged his nub of a tail, bounded after the ball, and returned it. Georgia patted his head. "Drop it."

"Good morning." Dr. Dave waved as he entered the play yard, two puppies nipping at his heels. "Want to trade?"

"No thanks. We're doing fine." Onyx licked her hand, the tacky slobber settling between her fingers. "Okay, two more balls, then I'll brush you. You'd like that, wouldn't you?" She threw the ball farther. He retrieved it but trudged back with an unsteady gait. Onyx appeared dazed and buried his face in Georgia's slacks. "What's wrong, fella?"

He dropped to the ground, eyes glazed over, teeth gnashing, and legs jerking.

Georgia gasped and balled up her hands at her mouth to squelch the scream trapped in her throat. Dr. Dave squatted. His mouth moved, but his words were incomprehensible. Her heartbeat hammered in her ears.

Onyx thrashed. Foamy saliva seeped between his clenched teeth. A gurgle escaped. A sound like the last sound she'd heard from William. Her hands covered her ears. She couldn't endure this again.

She ran into the building and made it into the bathroom before vomiting and crumpling to the floor. "Please don't die."

"Georgia?"

Her muscles tensed. She pressed her palms against her temples and refused to respond.

"Georgia, are you okay? It's Lani."

She couldn't hear what Lani had come to tell her. Onyx was surely dead. Georgia wailed. "I'm so sorry."

"Georgia, I'm coming in." Lani sat next to her and rubbed her back. "Can I help?"

"Is Onyx ..." Georgia shook her head and buried her face in her hands.

"I don't know. I'll check." Lani patted Georgia's knee and helped her to her feet. "Wait here."

Georgia glanced in the mirror. Locked the door. Pain gripped her chest; every inhalation was a shard in her heart. She rubbed her forehead, staring at the tile floor. "I'm no good to anyone."

The doorknob rattled. "Please let me back in."

Georgia fumbled with the lock. Dreaded the inevitable news.

Lani took her hands. Smiled. "Onyx is recovering but seems disoriented. Dr. Dave says he'll keep a close eye on him and run some tests. Would you like to see him?"

"I ... can't." Georgia bit the inside of her cheek. Looked away. "I don't want to upset him further."

"What do you mean, further?" Lani shook her head and squeezed Georgia's hands. "You didn't upset him, Georgia. He had a seizure."

Lani might be her best friend, but she hadn't been there. Hadn't heard the death gurgle or been there when William—she pressed her fingers against her temples—when Onyx fell at her feet. Lani wasn't the one who'd been paralyzed, unable to render assistance. "I can't see him, but I can't leave until I know he's settled. He must be so frightened."

"Okay. But you can't really wait in here."

Georgia struggled to find her voice. "How about your office?"

"I'm sorry. Today's the day the deep cleaning crew is in there." Lani touched Georgia's shoulder. "How about you go to the break room for a while? I need to take Mother for a doctor's appointment, but I'll ask Dr. Dave to let you know as soon as Onyx is alert."

Folding her arms across her chest, Georgia nodded.

Lani kissed her cheek. "I'll call you later."

"All right."

"And Georgia, try not to worry. Dr. Dave is doing everything he can."

"What if everything isn't enough?"

Done. Romel lowered the boom on the manlift and cleaned the primer from his spray gun. Now if those bozos down at the paint supply warehouse would just get his paint delivered. He mopped sweat from the back of his neck. It'd be nice to have this job done before the worst heat of summer hit. Besides, even though he was a volunteer, he'd agreed to have the job completed by July 30. He hadn't missed a deadline in thirty-three years, and he didn't plan to start now.

He poured paint thinner into the sprayer canister. Gagged. Romel had hated that odor since he first started painting houses. He never would've guessed when he started painting houses fresh out of the military that he'd still be at it at fifty-five. Well, still at it if they'd just deliver his dang paint.

Might as well head for the break room to eat lunch while he waited for his delivery. A striking brunette sat at the round table, swirling ice cubes in a glass of water, her pert nose speckled with red blotches, and glazed eyes dripping tears.

He opened the refrigerator door and lingered a minute in the cool air. "Mind if I sit down?"

"No." She brushed something from the front of her smock. "You go right ahead. I'm almost done."

Did she mean she was almost done with her water, or almost done working, or almost done crying? Best to be friendly. "I'm the painter. Name's Romel. Romel Bautista." He stuck out his hand. "Nice to meet you."

"Georgia Weber." She touched his palm. Managed a fleeting smile.

"What do you do here, Georgia Weber?" He took a bite of his ham and cheese on rye.

"I'm a volunteer."

"Me too. But just a temporary. Told Lani I'd paint the building." He paused. She didn't add to the conversation, so he continued. "What's your favorite part of the job?"

She wrung her hands. Stared at the table. "Working with the animals."

"I can see why. I've always loved animals. Have a parrot at my house. Bert's part of the family." He raked both hands through his hair and thought, "What's left of my family."

His phone rang. He dipped his chin and took the call. "What the devil do you mean you can't fill the order? I needed that paint yesterday."

He scratched his scalp. Glanced at Georgia. Told himself to calm down and not yell in front of the pretty lady.

"Look, Romel"—the paint guy sounded like a used car salesman—"I can get you a substitute. A new brand."

Romel's jaw tightened. He turned his back to Georgia. "Ten-year warranty?"

"I'll personally guarantee the product. You know you won't get this price anywhere else."

Romel smacked his lips. "What choice do I have? How soon can you deliver?"

"Four ... five days tops."

"All right." Romel snapped his phone shut and clicked his tongue. Dang it all. He was going to have trouble meeting his deadline now.

Georgia glanced at him. "Troubles?"

"Yeah."

"Seems to be going around today."

Romel sat back down at the table, took a bite of his sandwich, and studied Georgia. Should he ask about *her* troubles?

Before Romel could formulate a question, a man dressed in green scrubs strode in, sat down next to Georgia, and took her hand. "Onyx recognized me, I think. He's still groggy, but he stood. I'm sure he'd like to see you."

She shook her head. "He'll associate me with the trauma. I can't do that to him, Dr. Dave." Tears flooded her eyes and streamed down her cheeks. "I'm sorry I wasn't able to help him."

"Let's leave that in the past."

Georgia buried her face in her hands. "I wish I could."

CHAPTER TWO

GEORGIA SAT IN HER car at the animal shelter parking lot for several minutes. After thinking about it for five long days, she had to tell Lani she couldn't continue her duties at the shelter. Georgia gnawed at the inside of her cheek, clutched her purse, exited the car, and trudged toward the shelter. As she neared the manlift, she looked up. The painter—Romel wasn't it?—must have received his order. He was spraying blue paint.

Shoulders sagging, Georgia plodded toward Lani's office and eased into a chair. "I can't work with the animals anymore." Tears cascaded down her cheeks. She sucked in a breath, released it slowly, then shook her head. "I can't ... I can't be trusted to care for the animals. To care for *anyone*."

Lani walked around her desk and rubbed Georgia's back. "You're a volunteer, and I can't ask you to do anything you're not comfortable doing. But I'd sure hate to lose you."

"I thought Onyx was dying, and I just froze. I was no help at all. It's just like ..."

"Like what, sweetie? Like when William died?"

Georgia stared at her friend. "I'm trained to help. It should be second nature. I can't believe I was an emergency room nurse."

"I wish you could rid yourself of this guilt. Maybe you just need more time. I'd prefer not to lose you as a volunteer, and more importantly, I don't want my best friend to be home alone all day. What if you tried something different?"

"I love working here"—fresh tears soaked her tissue—"but I don't trust myself with the animals."

"I didn't mean stop volunteering at the shelter. I meant try something away from the animals for a while."

Georgia blew her nose, dabbed at her eyes, and sniffled. "What do you have in mind?"

"I need someone to head up the food booth committee for the Fourth of July celebration. It's only a little more than a month away. I can usually manage, although with Mother needing more attention these days and the grant applications due soon, I don't think I can finish organizing the committee. What do you think?" Lani cocked her head and raised her brows. "It would really help me out."

She couldn't say no to Lani. "I could try."

"Good. I'll give you my files and the list of volunteers who already agreed to serve on the committee. There might be a minor glitch with our menu. For the last three years, we served pulled-pork sandwiches, chips, and soda. The Hilo Gardening Club already signed up for pulled-pork sandwiches, so our committee will have to make another choice. I'll forward the email that lists all the food that's already approved." Lani shook her head. "Sorry about that."

"We'll come up with something. I'll get right on it." A distraction. Just what Georgia needed.

"You can work in the break room for now, or we could set you up in the corner of my office. There's probably a spare table around here somewhere." Lani dropped several files into an empty banker's box.

A little burst of optimism sparked in Georgia. At least she could be of use to someone. "I'll start in the break room today and see how it goes. Thanks."

"Thank you for helping me out of a jam. Let me know if you have any questions. And Georgia, please take care of yourself."

Georgia spread the files across the break room table. Fifteen committee members. Was that enough? They'd managed for seven years, so the number must work out okay. The applications for the Hawaii Department of Health were due in a week. She'd need to call a committee meeting right away. Lani always held fundraising meetings in her home. Georgia hadn't hosted guests in her home since moving to Hawai'i. Could she handle a supper meeting as soon as Friday?

Romel entered the break room and waved. He poured a couple of Tylenol into his hand and gulped them down with water. "Hello, Georgia. Feeling better?"

"Yes, thanks." Her hand flew to her hair and smoothed it down. "How about you?"

"I'm a happy camper. Finally got my paint."

"That's good."

Romel massaged his temples. "Looks like they're keeping you busy."

"I'm the new chair for the fundraising committee."

"Fundraising, huh?"

"Lani asked me to take over the Fourth of July food booth."

"That's coming right up." He munched on some carrots and celery sticks.

Georgia grinned. "Your wife must have you on a diet. I don't know that I've ever seen a man pack raw vegetables in a lunch."

Romel swallowed so hard his Adam's apple protruded and shifted up and down. "Packed it myself. Wife never did pack my lunches. Or fix my breakfast. She always made sure the kids had some food though, I'll say that for her. Made some attempt at cooking dinner for the family."

Past tense. Divorced, or was he widowed like her? She rummaged through the files, pulled out papers, and examined them. Put them back. Stole a glance at him.

His lips curled into a smile. She looked at her hands. A quiver started in her toes and raced to her fingers. She had no business thinking about any man except William. Yet, widowed or divorced, he was single, just like her, and maybe just as lonely. She met his gaze. Allowed a smile to emerge.

Romel could take a hint. Even though he wanted to know more about Georgia, he didn't want to disturb her while she worked. He quietly packed up the rest of his lunch. Lani came in with a gray-haired gal with glasses swinging from a multicolored lanyard.

"Aloha, Romel. This is my mother, Harriet." Lani pulled out a chair and helped her mother sit. "Mother, this is Romel. He's the man who volunteered to paint the building."

Harriet whipped her head toward him, a scowl creasing her forehead. "How long are you going to have that metal thing blocking the play yard?"

"Mother, he needs to reach the second story." Lani's voice was calm, and her eyes begged his patience. "We're fortunate Romel volunteered to paint the building and pay for the paint. It's very generous of him."

Harriet folded her arms across her chest. "*Humph.*"

Romel had dealt with lots of grumpy old folks. Always best to be kind. "If everything goes right, I'll be done in a few weeks." He flashed a smile her way. Thought about the five-day delay he'd just had, then said, "Hopefully by mid-July."

Georgia gathered her files and slipped them into the box. "I think I'll take you up on sharing your office, Lani. This table should be for breaks."

"Well, of course it should," Harriet spat. "This *is* the break room. Sometimes I think you lack all logic, Georgia."

"Mother, please. This was my idea, not Georgia's."

"Well, aren't you two a pair? Where's my lunch?" Harriet snapped the tab off a soda. "It's about time the color changes. I hate the green. Looks like an army barracks."

Lani shook her head and opened her mouth, but no words spilled out. Romel piped up, "The new paint is called Blue Mist."

"It even sounds pretty, doesn't it, Mother?"

Harriet grunted and bit into her sandwich.

"Georgia," Lani said. "I heard from Dr. Dave. He thinks he knows why Onyx had the seizure."

"Oh?" Georgia looked up, her hands gripping her coffee cup so tightly Romel thought it would crack. "Was it too much exercise?"

"They don't know what the trigger was—"

"I pushed him too hard. If I had paid closer attention ..." Her dimpled chin quivered, and the color drained from her face.

"Stop blaming yourself." Lani squeezed Georgia's hand. "Dr. Dave says it's because Onyx has some metabolic imbalance common in older dogs. You had no way of knowing that. You were doing what we recommend for all the dogs. They need exercise."

"Still ..." Georgia hung her head and dabbed at her eyes.

Harriet stared at her and clicked her tongue. "Maybe Onyx is not the only one who needs meds."

A little growl escaped Lani's throat. "Mother!"

"Pardon me." Georgia scrambled from the room.

Romel wasn't accustomed to a woman who was so sensitive. His ex-wife had tougher skin than most of the soldiers he'd known. "Will she be okay?"

"With time," Lani said.

Harriet's voice filled the room. "She's a nurse, for crying out loud. I wouldn't want her taking care of me, that's for sure!"

"Mother, please. Show some compassion. She's had a difficult time."

"I heard she didn't help Onyx at all. Did the same thing when her husband collapsed. Didn't help a bit."

Lani dipped her chin and rolled her shoulders.

Romel blew out his cheeks, then slowly released the air. Georgia sure had gone through some tough times.

Georgia set up extra folding chairs around her living room to accommodate the twelve fundraising committee members who had agreed to come to the meeting. When the phone rang, she assumed it'd be a committee member confirming directions to her house.

"Georgia?"

"Hi, Lani.

"Guess who asked to join the fundraising committee?"

"I give."

"Romel. The painter. I gave him your address. He was absolutely adorable when he came to my office to volunteer for your committee."

"Okay. I'll expect one more person."

"I think he likes you."

"Oh, for pity's sake, Lani. See you later."

Georgia laid her house phone in its cradle. Lani was wrong. This Romel guy just wanted to help out where he could. He was a volunteer. No different from any of the others who were helping with the food booth.

Still, she couldn't help but wonder if he was as lonely as she was.

CHAPTER THREE

ROMEL PARKED HIS MIDNIGHT blue panel truck on the street under the shade of a well-established plumeria tree as if hiding from the Mercedes and Volvos scattered around the neighborhood. This area was home to Hilo's professionals, while his neighborhood was blue collar all the way. He swore if he ever came into a lot of money, he'd offer to paint every house on his street.

He was fifteen minutes early—enough time to offer his help and maybe get to know a little more about Georgia before the others arrived. He marched up the front steps and rang the doorbell. She answered the door with a platter of cheese and crackers in one hand. Romel pointed at the tray. "Looks good."

"I hope so. Come in. We'll meet in there." She gestured toward the living room with her free hand.

"Need help?" It was the first time he'd seen her without her work smock. Her purple knit shirt stretched across her ample breasts in much the same way her matching Capri pants hugged her bottom. He appreciated a woman with a full figure. Georgia didn't disappoint him.

She shifted her weight from one foot to the other and scrunched her brow.

He offered more specific help. "I know my way around a kitchen pretty good."

She led the way. Her kitchen was three times the size of his, with modern stainless-steel appliances and copper pots and pans that hung from a decorative rack. Georgia jerked her head from side to side. She set down the platter and started wiping the counters.

He collected dirty dishes and carried them to the sink. She seemed especially nervous. He wondered if he was the reason.

"I'm so sorry"—she waved her hand in front of her face—"about this mess."

"Looks like my kitchen when I'm making pies. There's flour all over the place. Vacuums up pretty fast though."

She stopped scrubbing the marble countertops. "You bake pies?"

"Yep. It's my hobby. Relaxes me."

Georgia shook her head. "You're certainly more comfortable in the kitchen than most men I've known. My dad and husband barely knew where to find the juice glasses, let alone make a pie. Homemade crust and all?"

"Is there any other kind?"

The edges of her mouth rose, then plummeted as she glanced at her watch. Her hands fidgeted, and her gaze darted from counter to doorway. "They'll be here soon."

"Let's finish up then."

He carried pupu platters to the living room and moved a few photos on the side tables to make room. "Are these your kids?"

Georgia picked up a photo and pointed. "This is Samantha and her husband, Jim." She ran her fingers over the frame. "I'd like to see them more often, but they live in Iowa and only get so much vacation time from work."

"I don't see mine very often either. Tommy went to the military right out of high school. Met Dana in South Carolina. She owns a little shop and didn't want to leave there, so Tommy stayed. Princess is with my ex up in Los Angeles."

"Princess, huh? Before moving to Hawai'i, I'd only ever heard Princess as a nickname."

"The first time I saw her, I knew that little girl would always be my little princess. And Cynthia and I had an agreement that she could name our firstborn, and I could name our second. I wanted a Filipino name to honor my heritage. Princess seemed perfect." He bobbed his head. "Still is."

"How old is she?"

"Eighteen last month. Enrolled in a beauty school."

"Beauty school?"

"Wants to do make-up and hair for the stars." He rolled his eyes. "I think she just wants to be with her mama."

"Well, Samantha and Jim will come for the Fourth, so I'll get to see them soon."

"That's our plan too. The kids haven't been together since the divorce. I finally get to meet my son's fiancée."

Georgia opened the door to a group of committee members, including Harriet and Lani.

Romel offered his arm to Harriet. "Nice to see you again. Harriet, isn't it?"

"Of course, it's Harriet. You don't think I changed my name since you met me, do you?"

Lani scooted her mother toward the couch and engaged her in conversation. Thank goodness for Lani. Georgia was nervous enough about entertaining without having to deal with Harriet's rude comments.

The last to arrive was Auntie Lei, the former director of the shelter. She took a seat on the other side of Harriet and talked about the old days with her. Lani helped Georgia serve iced tea. "I'm so grateful for Auntie Lei. I swear Mother is only happy when she talks about the old days."

"It does seem that way." Georgia sighed. "Your mother is a handful."

"And unlike me, Auntie Lei knows how to make her smile."

Lani sat back down by her mother. "Aren't the stuffed mushrooms delightful, Mother?"

Harriet cleared her throat. "I thought we came here for a meeting."

"Yes. A supper meeting."

"It's dinner." Harriet glared. "No one calls it supper."

Georgia bit the inside of her cheek, attempting to ignore her. "Let's get started. Our primary business is to decide on a menu for the food booth. Evidently another group signed up for pulled-pork sandwiches."

"Do you know what other foods we *can't* serve?" Harriet snapped.

Georgia pasted on a smile. "I have the list right here. We can't serve hot dogs, hamburgers, pulled-pork sandwiches, falafel, funnel cakes, cotton candy, or ice cream."

"Well, that doesn't leave much, does it?" Harriet snarled.

Lani suggested they list the possibilities, and several reached into their pockets or purses and pulled out notepads. That was more like what Georgia had expected.

"Let's go around the room and everyone say something without discussion before we talk about the ideas," Romel said. "That's what we do at the Rotary meetings."

"We're not the Rotary." Harriet pursed her lips, but the others bobbed their heads. Georgia asked who wanted to start.

When no one offered, Romel suggested green salad. The lady next to him said corn dogs, and then in quick succession, the others named spam *musubi*, saimin, *loco moco*, and freshly squeezed lemonade. Georgia wrote down the ideas.

When it was her turn, she said she'd done some research, and "food-on-a-stick" was all the rage at fairs across the nation.

Harriet interrupted, "Like what?"

Her tone grated on Georgia's nerves, but she answered, "Like caprese salad."

"That's the stupidest idea I ever heard of. How can you put a salad on a stick?" Harriet clicked her tongue.

"I copied a photo to share." Georgia took a breath and tried to calm her jittery hands. She handed Harriet the photo.

"Look, Mother"—Lani pointed—"it looks like cherry tomatoes, mozzarella balls, and basil leaves."

"With an optional drizzle of balsamic vinaigrette," Georgia added.

"*Mmm, mmm.*" Romel rubbed his stomach.

Harriet clenched her hands in her lap.

Someone in the group said, "How about brownie bites on-a-stick?"

And then three voices in a row ended their suggestion with "on-a-stick." Everyone laughed except Harriet, who had crossed her arms in front of her chest and sat rigid as a post. Georgia's shoulders relaxed and settled into her chair. It was wonderful to have folks in her house having a lively conversation.

"Okay, we have an impressive list to discuss. Shall we eat our supper while we talk?" Georgia stood to go to the kitchen.

Harriet pushed herself to her feet. "I'm leaving. I don't care for any of your ideas, but I will help collect the money at the booth as long as I can stand the smell of whatever you decide!"

"Mother?" Lani grimaced. "Let's just sit down. I'm not ready to leave, and you don't have a ride home."

Harriet hobbled toward the door.

"Mother, wait. I'll drive you." Lani grabbed Georgia's hand. "I'm so sorry. She's been in such a bad mood lately. I'd better go."

Georgia closed the door behind her. Poor Lani, but supper was bound to be more enjoyable without Harriet. That old woman had a way of making Georgia feel bad about herself.

The group sat down to supper and discussed the pros and cons of the foods on the list and finally decided the caprese salad on-a-stick and a protein option would be reasonable. Italian sausage and green pepper skewers won out.

Each member signed up for a subcommittee. Romel said he'd take Harriet and Lani on his committee since they weren't there to speak for themselves. A few heads turned to him, mouths agape. One asked, "Are you sure?"

He just shrugged.

By the time Georgia served the red velvet cake, the conversation turned to the ongoing predicament at the animal shelter of finding adoptive homes for the older animals.

Someone mentioned she'd be glad to foster more dogs, but she was already over the limit allowed by her homeowner's covenants. Another man said he was in the same boat, and a third said she would love to take cats except her son was allergic. The woman to Georgia's right asked what type of pets she had.

Georgia looked at her plate and clasped her hands in her lap. "I ... I don't have any animals."

All eyes turned toward her. She felt as though she'd sprouted chicken legs and fairy wings.

Romel cleared his throat. "I don't want to be rude, but I wonder if I can get another cup of coffee?"

Georgia excused herself to the kitchen. Animals don't belong in the house. She heard William's voice as though he were standing next to her.

Romel lingered after the last committee member waved goodbye. He stacked the folding chairs while Georgia cleared the table. When he joined her in the kitchen, her face was red and blotchy across her nose and cheeks—just like the first time he had met her. Even at that, she was attractive, and not only physically. She cared deeply about animals. He could see that. And she cared what others thought about her. Maybe too much.

"Thank you for the help." Her voice was robotic. She turned her back to him and ran water in the sink.

"No problem. I think we have a good plan for the food booth, don't you?"

Georgia bobbed her head without turning around. Her shoulders shook, and she sniffled.

"I hope you're not upset about the supper conversation. Lots of people don't have pets."

"I love animals. I'd love to have pets, it's just that ..."

"What?"

The words rushed from her mouth in a deluge. "My husband didn't believe animals should be indoors. It would be disloyal to bring animals into his house."

Romel touched her arm. "This is your house too. If you want a pet, you should have one."

"I do want one. I want a house full of them. It's too darned quiet and lonely here. But I just can't." Georgia banged dishes together as she rinsed them in the sink.

Romel picked up a dishtowel and dried the coffee cups resting on the dish drainer. He kept silent. Words couldn't fix everything.

CHAPTER FOUR

ON MONDAY MORNING, GEORGIA arrived at the animal shelter early to get Lani's final approval and signatures for the fundraiser before she submitted the paperwork to the various agencies. Onyx was in the play yard with a new volunteer. A pang of guilt twisted Georgia's stomach. She should at least check to see how Onyx was doing. As soon as she entered the play yard, Onyx ambled up to her and dropped a ball at her feet. She reached down to pet his head. "Good dog. I'm sorry, Onyx. I don't have any treats."

The handler slipped a morsel of food into Onyx's mouth.

"How's he doing?" Georgia ran her fingers across the familiar arch of Onyx's back.

"Better now that *I'm* taking care of him." The young handler thrust her chin upward, crossed her arms over her flat chest, and glared.

Who was this snippy young woman? "Should he be chasing a ball so soon after his seizure?"

The young volunteer put her hands on her hips. "Dr. Dave recommended it."

"Oh."

Onyx sidled up to the young woman. "If I could have pets in my apartment building, I'd so take him home."

Guilt percolating in her shoulders, Georgia left the play yard. Once inside Lani's office, she relaxed enough to report to Lani that the committee had decided on the caprese salad on-a-stick and sausage and pepper skewers.

"Sounds yummy." Lani signed the applications, snapped the folder shut, and handed the packet back to Georgia. "Did Romel behave himself?"

Georgia swatted at Lani with the folder. "I'm sure I don't know what you mean."

"Come on. You have to admit he's a good-looking guy."

"And he's just as nice as can be, but for pity's sake, Lani, it's not like he asked me out or anything."

"Not yet. I bet he will."

"Stop it." Heat skittered across Georgia's face. She fanned herself with a folder. "On another note, is it still okay to set up a table in here?"

"Sure thing." Lani rummaged in a storage closet and handed out a card table and a chair. "You'll probably want a cushion for this. Can't say I'd want to sit in a folding chair for very many minutes a day."

"I'll bring one from home. Thanks for sharing your office."

"No problem. It might be nice to have a human to talk to." As if on cue, Trudy squawked and flapped her bright red wings. "No offense, Trudy."

Georgia tapped the turtle terrarium on the edge of Lani's desk. "Do you think Franklin will mind?"

"He's not saying."

Once Georgia had her corner of the office set up, it occurred to her she'd have fewer chances to see Romel now that she wasn't in the break room.

Why did that matter anyway? He was just a nice man who happened to be on the same committee. Georgia grabbed her purse and told Lani she'd be right back after she dropped off the paperwork.

She veered to the east when she left the building to glimpse the manlift. No Romel today. Why did she feel disappointed?

When she returned, Georgia set a small basket of goodies on Lani's desk.

Lani's eyes widened. "Gee, thanks. What's this for?"

"For sharing your space with me."

"Looks delicious." Lani popped a chocolate truffle into her mouth, closed her eyes, and moaned. *Mmm.* "Divine. By the way, Romel called while you were out."

Georgia's stomach flipped. She grabbed the corner of her blouse and twisted. "Oh?"

Lani giggled, then raised her eyebrows. "He wanted to know what hours you worked."

"Why would he want to know that?" She bit the inside of her cheek.

"I don't know. Maybe he wants to arrange his volunteer hours around yours."

"For pity's sake, Lani." Her limbs tingled. "Did you tell him?"

"I did. I hope it's okay since you're on the same committee." Lani scrunched up her nose. "Did I screw up? I didn't give him your phone number."

"You didn't screw up. And he can have my phone number. Everyone else on the committee does."

Georgia floated back to her table. She hoped Lani was right. Maybe Romel did want to know her hours in order to see her more often. As flattering as that thought was, she wasn't ready to entertain the idea of allowing another man into her life.

She pulled out her powder compact and stared into the little mirror. It was going to take a lot of make-up to cover the crimson streaks that moved up her neck and settled on her cheeks.

"Good morning, everyone." The next morning, Georgia fed Trudy some sunflower seeds and stroked her feathers. Turning to Lani, she asked, "Anything new?"

"The approvals arrived from the Department of Health." Lani tilted her head toward Franklin's terrarium. "Don't you worry about making Franklin jealous?"

Georgia produced a cabbage leaf from her bag and set it next to him. "I didn't forget, did I, Franklin?"

"You spoil them."

"I need someone to spoil. Might as well be these two."

"What you need is a man to spoil." Lani teased, then lowered her voice. "And here's one now."

Georgia spun around. Romel stood in the office doorway, baseball cap clasped in his hands like a kid who'd been called to the principal's office.

"Morning." He shifted his weight from one foot to the other. "I wonder if I could talk to you about a problem on my subcommittee?"

"Sure. Have a seat."

He stayed put. "Could we talk in the hallway?"

Georgia's heart thumped in her throat. They walked a few feet from the office.

Romel licked his lips. "Would you like to eat supper with me?" Words poured from his mouth like a burst of fireworks. "To discuss a problem on my subcommittee? I have some chicken adobo and vegetables in my Crockpot and a homemade macadamia nut pie in the fridge."

He probably wanted to discuss Harriet and didn't want to talk about Lani's mother at the shelter. It should be safe to go to his house. They would be alone, but it was a business meeting, and he was an upright citizen from all accounts.

She raised her eyebrows. "Macadamia nut pie, huh? Who can say no to that?"

His shoulders relaxed and he sported a cockeyed grin. "I'll pick you up at five-thirty."

Georgia bobbed her head. "That's fine."

"It's a date."

A date? *Hmm.* The edges of her lips crept upward. He hadn't called it a business meeting. Her smile faded. Would Samantha think it was too soon after her dad's death? *Was* it too soon? Georgia's brow tightened. Romel hadn't meant an actual date. It would simply be two adults discussing committee business and sharing supper, wouldn't it?

Georgia peered at her reflection and applied extra powder over the redness that seemed to creep from her neck to her cheeks every time she even thought about Romel. She touched the gray hairs at her temples, attempting to tuck them under her dark-brown hair. Should she color her hair? Nonsense. The man already knew she was graying. Anyway, it wasn't like this was a real date. Regardless of what Romel had called it, the only reason they were meeting outside the shelter was to discuss the problem with Harriet in private.

Five-sixteen. Romel would arrive soon. She freshened her mascara and lipstick and forced herself to leave the mirror. She sat in her recliner and leafed through the pages of *Better Homes and Gardens*.

A beam of reflected light crawled up the wall. He was in the driveway. She peeked through the Venetian blinds. He was early, just as he'd been for the committee meeting. Georgia walked toward the front door, thought better of it, and went to the kitchen to run some cool water over her wrists. Her house was air-conditioned. Why on earth did she feel so hot?

Romel wrapped up work earlier than usual to go to the barber. His military crew cut looked sharp—at least he thought so. He showered, shaved, applied a splash of aftershave and an extra swipe of antiperspirant. On the drive over, he stopped at a florist shop for a bouquet of pink anthuriums, king protea, and bird-of-paradise. He'd never paid that much for flowers in his life, but this was his first date since his divorce, and he wanted to do it right.

He pulled into the driveway, turned off the engine, and dragged his fingers across his scalp. Should he hold the flowers behind his back or just hand them to her when she opened the door?

He saw Georgia look out the window. "What in the world is wrong with you?" he muttered to himself. "Get out of the truck."

On the lanai, he held the flowers behind his back and pushed the doorbell. Georgia opened the door, her voluptuous body framed by the threshold. The sight of her rendered him tongue-tied. He thrust the flowers toward her. "I ... I hope you have a vase."

Georgia fumbled with the flowers and looked down.

"Something wrong? Are you allergic to them?" Romel crunched his forehead.

"No, they're beautiful. I wasn't expecting ... it's just that ... never mind. Thank you." She stepped from the threshold. "Come in. I'll just go put these in water."

He pulled his baseball cap from his head as she disappeared into the kitchen. Jeez! He didn't want her to think he didn't have any manners.

She emerged a few minutes later with the flowers arranged in a bright blue watering can.

"They're lovely, Romel. I'll just put them on the dining room table. I'm ready."

Romel fumbled in his pocket for his handkerchief, wiped his brow, and took a deep breath.

Chapter Five

Georgia locked the front door and walked beside Romel to the passenger side of his panel truck. He offered her his hand as she stepped up and settled herself on the seat. A quick look at her face in the side-view mirror confirmed her cheeks were scarlet. As Romel got in the driver's seat, she pulled the seatbelt across her stomach. It wasn't long enough to latch. Her belly was bloated. Perspiration trickled from her temples. She tried again. Still too short.

"Oh, sorry about that." He jumped from the truck and ran around to her side. "I should have mentioned, it helps to pull it forward as far as you can reach and then swing it back to buckle it. Like this." He grabbed the buckle and pulled the belt toward the windshield—she sucked in a breath and tightened her tummy as much as was possible these days. He reached across her to latch it. His arm rested on her belly. He jiggled the buckle. "Dang thing."

"Hold on." He let the belt rewind, stepped up to the floorboard, and started the process all over. With one hand on the headrest, he leaned across her, his chin grazing her left arm. She shifted her hips. *Click.*

She exhaled with a *whoosh*. He scrambled away, red-faced and jerking his head from side to side. "I probably should replace that."

On the drive, Romel fussed with everything from the air conditioner fan to the mirrors. Neither spoke until they pulled into a double car garage so full of ladders and painting supplies his panel truck barely fit.

"We're here." He jumped out and scrambled to the passenger side. Thank goodness she was able to unlatch the seat belt before he opened her door. She was capable of opening doors herself——Lord knew she did it all the time——but she still appreciated Romel's old-fashioned manners. It didn't make her feel less powerful, as her daughter claimed. It made her feel cared for. She missed that feeling.

Once they were in his house, Romel recovered his voice. He introduced Georgia to his parrot and asked Bert to say hello. Bert let out a catcall whistle followed by "kiss her quick."

Georgia giggled. When was the last time anyone whistled at her? "Who taught him that?"

Romel shook his head. "It's a funny story. Princess taught him that about the time my son started dating. Poor Tommy. Every time he invited a girl over, Bert whistled and called out 'kiss her quick.'"

"Poor kid. He must have been so embarrassed." Georgia clicked her tongue and wagged her finger at Bert.

Romel added, "Tommy hated it, but he loves Bert."

"He's beautiful. How old?"

"About twenty-five, I guess. After I took over the painting business, one of my first clients had some unexpected medical bills. He asked if I'd be willing to take part of my payment in trade, and I agreed. He owned a pet store, and I got to go in and pick out any animal I wanted."

"I used to have Trudy, the macaw in Lani's office, at my house. When we built the house, I asked for an aviary. I figured an outdoor space in this climate would work well and there would be no pets indoors to upset William." The words caught in her throat. She whisked a tear from her cheek and sighed. "It didn't work out."

She should stop talking, and she certainly should stop crying. Romel would think she cried all the time. And he wouldn't be wrong.

He didn't comment. Just gazed at her until she looked away.

"Kiss her quick." Bert paced the length of his perch.

Romel chuckled. "I think I might know how Tommy felt."

"And I might know how his girlfriends felt."

Romel ran his hands through his hair. Georgia turned her attention to a shelf filled with family photos. "Good-looking kids."

He perked up. Pointed to one of the photos. "This is Tommy and his fiancée, Dana."

"And the one in the tutu must be Princess." There were lots of photos of her compared to Tommy.

"Yep, she'll always be my little girl."

"I know the feeling. I have trouble thinking of Samantha as a woman." She giggled. "She's old enough now to want to give *me* advice."

"Like what?"

"She wants me to move back to Iowa."

"Have you considered that?"

"I have. But living in Hawai'i was a lifelong dream. I can't abandon the house William built for us." She blinked back tears. "I'm sorry. I shouldn't talk about my husband with you."

"It's okay. Really." He stepped closer to her. Cocked his head. "You can talk about him all you like. If he's the reason you moved to Hawai'i, then I'm forever indebted to him."

Heat radiated from her chest to her cheeks. Romel closed the gap between them. Cradled her cheek in his palm. She looked at the floor and stepped away. "I'd like to freshen up."

Romel scraped his hands through his hair. "Sorry about that, Georgia."

"It's just—"

"You don't need to explain. The bathroom is down the hall, first door on the right."

Had she given him the wrong impression by agreeing to come to his house? She had no experience with men other than William. Georgia chided herself—get a grip. It's not like she was in danger; she wasn't even desirable. She was overweight, red-faced, and teary-eyed. Breathing deeply, she counted to ten. She'd march right back out there and remind him why she'd come—to discuss the problem on his committee.

He still stood in the same spot she'd left him. His face still apologetic. His embarrassed voice an attempt to smooth things over. "How about we eat supper so we can get to that pie?"

Her shoulders relaxed. "And we can talk about the problem on your committee."

"Right." He led her to the dining room, pulled out her chair, and snapped a linen napkin onto her lap. "I'll go get the food."

He set a beautifully plated supper dish in front of her. The savory aroma of garlic and something she couldn't identify filled her nostrils. "Smells delicious."

"It's the bay leaves. Found the recipe in a box from my mama's house. She used to make this for Sunday dinner."

They ate without talking until the silence became too much for her. "Is Harriet the problem on your committee?"

He stopped—a forkful of vegetables suspended between his plate and his mouth—and licked his lips. "About that—"

"The thing about Harriet is that we need to tolerate her, for Lani's sake, but tell me what she's done."

"It's not Harriet." He set his fork down, planted his elbows on the table, and clasped his hands together. "I have to be honest with you."

"Do you want off the committee?"

"No. There's not a problem." He gazed at her, a sheepish grin emerging. "I made it up."

"I don't understand. Why would you make up a problem?"

"Because it was the only way I could think of to get you to have supper with me."

"I see." So, he *did* consider this a date. She hid her budding smile behind her hand.

"I hope you're not angry. I just wanted to get to know you better and see if you liked my pie." He waggled his eyebrows.

"Okay. I'm glad there isn't a problem. We can talk about other things."

"Okay"—he held up his right hand, palm facing out—"from now on, I promise to tell the truth, the whole truth, and nothing but the truth."

Her smile reached across her face.

Romel tapped the table twice. "Let's start over. How long have you been in Hawai'i?"

"Six years. We were both able to take early retirement. Since the first time we dropped off Samantha at the University of Hawai'i, we knew we wanted to live in the state and found every excuse to visit her. We liked O'ahu but preferred the quieter pace of Hawai'i Island. We spent years designing and saving for our retirement home."

"It's a beautiful home."

"It is. William used to tease that he loved the house almost as much as he loved Samantha and me."

"Too bad he didn't get much time to enjoy it."

She swiped a tear and changed the subject. "How many buildings do you paint a year?"

"It depends on the square footage and how much prep work I need to do before I paint. Then there's the weather."

"So many variables. I don't know how you have time to paint the shelter for free."

"Well, it's something I can contribute. I've been able to slip in a few hours every week between my other commitments. The biggest headache for the shelter is to have the manlift platform up for so many weeks, but a two-story building demands it."

"The manlift is a small price to pay for a fresh coat of paint. The building was looking pretty run-down."

He jumped up from the table. "Ready to try my pie?"

"I can't wait." She pushed out her chair. "Let me help clear the table."

"Next time."

Next time?

He set a piece of pie in front of her and waited at her side. She admired the perfect ratio of filling to macadamia nuts. The texture was perfection—creamy custard and flaky crust—and the taste extraordinary. "It's superb!"

His head bounced up and down. "Good, because I plan to make a mango pie this weekend. Will you come over to try it?"

"Saturday?" she blurted.

"It's a date."

"Bring the pie to my house. I'll make supper."

Georgia took her last bite of the sweet filling and smiled. A second date within a week. Someone to fill the lonely evening hours. She didn't know what she'd done to deserve this man's attention.

CHAPTER SIX

"GOOD MORNING, LANI." GEORGIA removed a plastic bag from her purse and set it down on her table.

Trudy fluffed her feathers. "Pretty bird."

"Step up." Georgia extended her fingers, and Trudy landed on them, then stepped up to ride on Georgia's shoulder.

"She loves you," Lani said. "Don't you, Trudy?"

Trudy squawked and rubbed her beak against Georgia's scalp. "Here's your treat." Georgia fed her an apple chunk. "Go to your perch."

Trudy obeyed and received an additional treat. Georgia retrieved a cabbage leaf from the bag and dropped it into Franklin's terrarium.

"You're in a cheerful mood this morning." Lani looked at Georgia sideways. "Does a certain painter have anything to do with that?"

"Why would you ask that? Can't I just be in a good mood?"

"You can. But I suspect there's something you're not telling me."

Georgia beamed. "I had supper with Romel last night. Please don't say a word to anyone."

"Told you he'd ask you out. It must have gone well. I haven't seen you this chipper in a very long time."

"He's easy to talk to."

Lani wiggled her eyebrows. "Just talk?"

"Stop." Georgia slapped at Lani's arm. "Of course, it was just talk. For pity's sake."

The phone on Lani's desk jangled. She held the receiver to her ear and drew her eyebrows together. "Bring them right over."

"What's going on?"

"That was animal rescue. They shut down a puppy mill and have eleven Doberman pups that need emergency medical care. I'll text Dr. Dave, but would you be able to stay and assist?"

Georgia wrung her hands. Could she? "I'll stay, but you know I'm not good in an emergency."

"But you know medical procedures. This new group of interns might need more supervision than Dr. Dave can manage."

Before Georgia could respond, an animal rescue worker knocked on Lani's door and asked her to sign for the eleven Dobies in the hallway. Georgia and Lani followed the worker to the two cages. Georgia gasped, then gagged. The pups' tails were a mangled mess of rotting flesh.

Lani kneeled beside the cages and held her hand over her nose and mouth. "We only have room for four. We need to free up some space. I'll call our list of fosters and see if anyone would be willing to house a dog or two for the next month to make room for these little guys. Would you mind prepping the lab?"

Georgia wanted to help, but the pups looked extremely fragile. Could she trust herself to tend to them? She bit her lip and looked from the struggling creatures to Lani's hopeful expression. "Sure."

"That'd be great." Lani stood. "Oh, hello Romel."

Georgia got to her feet. Romel stood behind them, his nose covered with his kerchief. "Good Lord. What happened?"

"Some idiot bungled an attempt to clip their tails and evidently didn't even know to feed them properly."

"Poor little things. Anything I can do to help?"

Lani shook her head. "Not unless you can take a few older dogs home today to make room for these little guys."

Romel scratched his head. "I could make a temporary shelter for these guys in the hallway. It'd just take a few sticks of lumber and some chicken wire to contain them."

"Mahalo." Lani disappeared into her office.

Dr. Dave and three vet students huddled around the Dobies. "Dehydration. Malnutrition. Infection." Dr. Dave held up a limp, smelly pup. "What do we do first?"

"Hydrate and start antibiotics through an intravenous drip." It was the sassy young woman from the play yard. She wasn't a volunteer like Georgia, she was one of Dr. Dave's students.

"That's right, Jennifer. I'll be back shortly. Georgia here is an RN. She'll take charge while I'm with Lani since you've never done these procedures on live animals before." He spun on his heels and headed toward the office.

Georgia hesitated. How could he trust her after what happened with Onyx? She'd assisted him lots of times with IV drips, but that was before ...

"Well,"—Jennifer stood akimbo, her tone brazen—"are you going to show us where to find the supplies?"

Georgia chewed on the inside of her cheek. Her feet refused to move. Romel touched her elbow and flashed her a smile. It was enough to spur her on. Was she going to let this intern rattle her? "Follow me."

She led the entourage into the lab and handed out surgical masks and gloves, then pulled tubing, needles, and bags of antibiotic solution from the cabinets. Compassion for the pups' welfare drove her concentration as she demonstrated how to prep the injection site and secure the catheter. Two of the interns teamed up and started the process, leaving Jennifer without a partner. Was she always the odd person out?

Georgia forced a smile. "I'll partner with you, Jennifer. Why don't you fetch one of the pups, and I'll hold her while you prep the injection site?"

Jennifer mumbled something, then retrieved a pup. She held her at arm's-length. "How long will they stink? I think I'm going to be sick."

"For a few days." Georgia took the pup.

Jennifer's surgical mask could not disguise her ashen face, nor could the gloves disguise her trembling hands. Georgia walked her through the process of cleansing the site and shaving the hair. "It's time to insert the needle."

Jennifer's green eyes widened. She picked up the needle. Dropped it. Her gaze darted around the room.

Without a word, Georgia handed the pup back to Jennifer and inserted the intravenous line. Jennifer glared at her. "Thanks for making me look bad."

Georgia didn't know what this girl's problem was, but Dr. Dave had asked her to instruct, so that's what she was trying to do. "Do you want to try on the next one?"

"No. If you're so good at it, you do it so I can get out of here."

Before they finished with the next pup, Auntie Lei poked her head through the doorway and offered to help. Jennifer slapped her gloves on the countertop. "You can take my place. I've had enough of this Know-It-All."

Auntie Lei shook her head, slipped on gloves and a mask, and held a pup. "Someone needs an attitude adjustment."

Georgia sighed. "It appears she doesn't like me. I'm not sure what to do about that."

"Are you asking for advice or just venting?"

"Both!"

"When people treat me disrespectfully, I'd like to think they are having a bad day and that it really has nothing to do with me."

"Evidently, she feels I made her look bad in front of her classmates. I was just trying to do what Dr. Dave asked of me." Tears gathered and threatened to spill over her cheeks. She brushed them away as casually as she could muster. "I shouldn't have agreed to be responsible for the interns, especially when they all seem to know I failed at taking care of Onyx."

Auntie Lei's gaze seared into her. "You listen to me. Dr. Dave trusted you with that responsibility, and from the looks of it, the other interns responded appropriately. I think this young woman has some issues, as the kids would say."

"I suppose you're right."

"I wouldn't steer you wrong. Now, while we finish up, tell me how Samantha is doing."

The change of subject suited Georgia just fine. She loved to brag a little about her only child, and she knew Auntie Lei loved to do the same about her niece. While they chatted, the two remaining interns said they had to get back to campus for class, but all the pups had their intravenous lines in place. "That was the first time we got to work on live animals. It feels good to know we helped."

As they walked away, one said, "Can you believe Jennifer walked out? Dr. Dave is going to be so mad."

Auntie Lei raised her eyebrows. "Now there's two young people who know how to appreciate an opportunity."

"That's the truth," Georgia agreed.

Romel joined Georgia and Auntie Lei at the cleaning station, rolled up his sleeves, and donned a pair of rubber gloves. "Looks like you could use some help."

"You can take my place. I should be going." Auntie Lei hugged Georgia and promised to meet again soon.

"Thank you, Auntie," Georgia said. She handed a little female to Romel. He cradled the pup in his arms and soothed her with his voice. As soon as Georgia started to clean her infected tail, yelping ensued and brought on a mournful serenade from the litter.

"You're gonna feel so much better when this pretty lady gets you all cleaned up," Romel told the pup.

Georgia stopped cleaning and smiled. When was the last time anyone called her pretty lady?

By the time Lani and Dr. Dave came into the lab, Romel and Georgia had finished cleaning the wounds. Dr. Dave said his afternoon shift of interns would take over from there. Romel snapped off his gloves and said he'd share his lunch if anyone was interested in a pretty good sandwich.

Georgia glanced at Lani, who raised her eyebrows and grinned. "You two go ahead. I'll eat with Mother later."

In the break room, Romel spread out his offerings.

"Are we still on for tomorrow at your place?" Romel looked up from his sandwich. "There's something I want to discuss with you."

"Yes. Tomorrow still works for me, but if you want to discuss something ..." Georgia felt a little hitch in her stomach. She wondered if he thought they should speed things up.

"I'd rather wait until we're alone." Romel reached across the table and squeezed her hand, then stood and cleaned up the table. "If you don't need any more help, I think I'll go buy materials to house the pups. See you tomorrow then."

Georgia fretted all day Saturday. She liked Romel. And she was quite sure he liked her. But what if he expected her to go to bed with him? Isn't that what people did these days? Jump into bed with people they barely knew. Good Lord, the only man who'd ever seen her naked was her husband. She liked the way things were right now. Someone to eat with and talk to. A companion. That's all he was to her. A companion. Right?

By late afternoon, she was so worked up she considered canceling. Did she trust him? What did she really know about this guy? Without thinking, she'd invited him to her house, where it would be difficult to send him home if things went sour. She should have let him host and driven herself over there.

By the time Romel arrived, there was no disguising her red-hot cheeks. She served him a glass of iced tea, sat across from him, and blurted, "What did you want to discuss?"

Romel scrubbed his hands through his crew cut and smacked his lips together.

Uh-oh, here it comes.

"I hate to ask for favors, but remember I told you my son is bringing his fiancée for the Fourth?"

She nodded.

He talked faster. "Tommy called the other night to say his gal just finished a barrage of allergy testing and it seems she's allergic to bird dander. I want her to be comfortable when she comes to visit, so I wondered ... if it's not too much to ask ..."

Georgia pressed her palm to her heart. A shaky laugh escaped her throat. "Are you asking me to house Bert?"

"Yep. You're the only one I can think of who has a good place for him to stay out of trouble without caging him all weekend in my basement. And even at that, my son's gal—"

"I'd love to." She'd been so silly to let her imagination run wild. Romel was nothing more than a friend who needed a favor.

"I thought I remembered you had an aviary." Romel grinned at her.

"I do. I mean, the room was designed as an aviary, but I've used it more recently as storage for garden supplies."

"Could I clean it up?"

"Okay. Sure. Do you have time tomorrow? We could do it together."

"How about three? I want to get the cages for the pups finished in the morning."

"Great."

Romel stood and offered his hand to help her up. "Now, what do you say we eat a slice of that pie *before* our supper?"

CHAPTER SEVEN

GEORGIA CALLED HER DAUGHTER on Sunday morning. She had to bite her tongue when Samantha off-handedly asked her if she'd gone on any dates lately. Georgia simply said, "You know me."

Later, she grinned that she'd been clever enough to avoid a direct answer. How was it that Romel made her feel like a young woman again? She hadn't been this giddy since … well, since William courted her.

By the time Romel arrived, she'd made potato salad and a raw vegetable plate and gone to the store for two nice rib eye steaks. She grabbed a carton of mocha almond fudge ice cream at the last minute in case Romel did not show up with one of his homemade pies.

He was ten minutes early. As usual. She opened the door and reached for the pie carrier. "Is this the mango pie?"

"Yep."

She invited him in. "How often do you bake pies?"

"Every weekend."

"That's a lot of pie!" She wondered if he always made sure he had a woman to share it with. "How do you stay so slim?"

"I enjoy baking them, but I only eat one or two pieces a week. Give the rest to the neighbors."

Of course he did. The corners of her mouth crept up. She barely knew him, yet he made her smile so naturally.

"I'll set this down and then we can take a look at the aviary before we eat."

She led him through the den and into the adjoining aviary.

"Here it is. Storage for my gardening supplies these past few years." Georgia sighed. "What do you think?"

"It's perfect."

"Will it be cool enough?"

"It'll be great." He looked beyond her. "I don't think we even have to remove your supplies. Maybe we can just stack them to one side. Bert's paper-trained, so he won't stain anything."

"Okay, then. We'll work on it after we eat." He followed her to the kitchen where she handed him a spatula and a plate with two steaks. "There's a gas grill out back. Do you mind doing the honors?"

After setting the table, she joined Romel in the backyard. It seemed as natural as a sunrise to watch him cook steaks on her grill. But she still didn't know much about him, and she was curious about so many things. "What made you go into the painting business?"

"It's all I knew when I got home from military duty. I'd worked for a painting outfit all through high school, so I knew what to do. Mr. Masters hired me back on, and when he retired, he offered to sell me the business. By that time, I was married and owning a business seemed like a good idea for job security."

"Any regrets?"

"Some. I knew how to paint, but running a business was a whole other story. I took some business classes at the community college and hired a bookkeeper to keep the records straight. It's worked out okay." He leaned forward. "How about you? You're an RN, right?"

"Was. I haven't worked in the field since we moved to the island."

"Any regrets?"

"Not many. I guess I wish I'd kept up my license so I could go back to work if I wanted, but I'm fortunate I don't have to work. That gives me more time to volunteer. And I love my work at the animal shelter."

"Yeah, it has to be rewarding to work around the animals all day. It's a great shelter."

"Lani does an excellent job managing the place."

"Did you have animals around the house when you grew up?"

"Everywhere! My mom brought home a lot of the injured animals from the rescue league. We even had an alligator once."

"An alligator?" His expression was priceless. "I love animals, but I don't think I'd want to be around a gator."

"When I went off to college, I had to leave my Dobie at my parents' house. As soon as I could move from the dorm, I fetched her. Asta was my constant companion all through nursing school."

"And then you got married."

"And then I married William, and he wasn't as fond of animals as I'd thought. I insisted on an apartment that allowed pets. Asta was a sweetie, but having her caused mayhem for our relationship, so I took her back to my parents."

"That was a long time ago. Any pets since that?"

"Only Trudy. And I already told you she ended up in Lani's office."

He tilted his head but didn't comment.

"I took her back to the shelter a month after bringing her home. She was all William could see when he was in his den, which was much of the time. And he swore he could hear her talking through the glass. I loved that about her—still do—that she's such a talker." She sighed and brushed her hair from her brow. "At least I get to see her at the shelter. Lani promised she wouldn't let her be adopted."

"That's a good friend."

"She's the best. Took me under her wing from the minute I volunteered. Funny thing is, it was William's idea for me to volunteer there so I could be around animals without him having to. Turns out it's been a godsend for me."

He nodded, continued his silence. Words poured from Georgia's mouth. "I'm making him sound like a control freak. He wasn't, you know." The familiar tears pooled and escaped down her cheeks. It was a mystery to her why she had this compulsion to defend William to Romel.

Romel reached for her hand. "He just sounds like a guy who wasn't crazy about animals. Not everyone is."

"That's right." Her chin trembled, and she dabbed at her wet cheeks. "Not everyone is."

Georgia was beautiful, even when she was upset. Romel loved that she didn't hide her feelings from him. She was so genuine compared to his ex-wife, who would claim he should know what was wrong without her telling him, like he was one of those clairvoyants at a street fair.

He waited until Georgia was composed, then changed the subject. "Tell me about your daughter."

The strain melted from her face. "Samantha is a lot like Lani. She has a great sense of humor and married a guy who is just as funny. She's a dance instructor. Met Jim in a salsa class." Georgia gazed into the distance, a glint in her eyes. "She's a joy to be around. I miss her, but it's not too much longer until they visit for the Fourth."

"I can't wait to meet them."

"How about your daughter? How long has she been in L.A.?"

"Two and a half years."

"Sounds like your house is just as lonely as mine."

"Could be better, I suppose. But then you go on with your life and pretty soon the empty house seems normal."

"Not to me. As much as I like a little time to myself, I'd love to have more activity in the house. I always thought William and I would spend our retirement years together." She shook her head slowly. "Then he died because ... he died prematurely."

"I'm so sorry you were left alone." He scraped his fingers across his scalp. "Bert helps me. We don't exactly have conversations, but he's a familiar presence just the same." Romel grinned. "Did I tell you Bert can make a sound exactly like a creaky door opening?"

"No."

"When Princess was eight, Cynthia organized a slumber party for her birthday. She hadn't heard Bert's new sound. In the middle of the night, he made the creaking door sound and scared the bejesus out of the girls."

He loved Georgia's hardy laugh. "Oh, those poor little girls. That is so funny, though."

"He's been a part of the family for a long time. In fact, I have one more favor to ask of you."

"Yes?"

"Would you mind if Princess and Tommy come to visit Bert while he's staying with you?"

"I'm sure we can work that out."

Romel slapped his hands to his knees. "Speaking of Bert, we'd better clean up our supper dishes and get going on the aviary before it gets any later."

Perspiration gathered on Georgia's upper lip as they worked side by side to stack the garden supplies along one wall of the aviary. She hoisted a twenty-pound bag of steer manure to her shoulder. The bag split open on impact—fertilizer settled on her clothes and covered her arms. *Ugh!* She tried to brush off the offending material, but her damp hands caused a tacky slurry to form on the hair of her forearms. She had to get out of there and freshen up.

Romel laid a hand on her elbow and turned her around. He dabbed her face with his handkerchief, then held her chin in his hand. The corners of his mouth lifted lazily. His gaze fixed on hers.

Her knees threatened to desert her. She bit the inside of her cheek. He was so close she wasn't sure where to look. She was sticky with perspiration and smelled of manure. How could he stand to be near her? William always insisted she shower as soon as she came in from gardening; he wouldn't come near her until after she was clean.

Romel's fingers grazed her lips, lingered there. His eyes questioning. Waiting. She wasn't ready to kiss him. Not like this. She was a mess.

Little quakes raced through her body, jeopardizing her resolve. She flattened a hand against his chest, his heartbeat racing under her palm, and dropped her chin.

He sucked in a breath and stepped away.

The space between them cooled. What was she doing? She wanted to kiss him. If this was her only chance to feel his lips on hers, she should take it, shouldn't she?

He turned toward the door.

"Wait." She caressed his cheek, peered into his gray eyes. She could trust him. Georgia draped her dirty arms around his neck and gently tugged. He settled his hands at the small of her back, his grin an invitation. She pressed her lips to his.

He deepened the kiss, then stepped back a little and moved his hands to cup her face. "I've been wanting to kiss you since the first time we met." He drew out the words. "That was nice."

She melted into him. "Nice enough for another?"

When he finished with her lips, he kissed her forehead. "I'm going to stop now before we do something we might regret."

They finished cleaning up the aviary in near silence. He hadn't meant to make Georgia uncomfortable around him. He shouldn't have started anything by initiating a kiss. But, dang it, he wanted to kiss her. And those two kisses were unbelievable and served to cement his feelings about her being the one for him. Remarkable. He'd never believed in love at first sight, yet here he was. He wouldn't take advantage of her vulnerability and risk messing up what they had so far. And when the time was right, he wanted to wake up next to her every morning.

He should say something. Make sure things were okay between them before he left. "Bert's going to feel right at home in here."

She faced him. "I hope so."

"About before"—he scraped his hands through his hair—"do you want to talk about it before I go home?"

"I'm sorry I got carried away."

"You?" He narrowed the distance between them.

"I'm so embarrassed. I'm flattered that you'd even want to be close to me when I'm such a mess." She spoke as if trying to convince herself. "I should be content to share suppers. Have a companion to talk to."

She'd misunderstood him. Glistening tears dripped down her cheeks. He opened his arms and cocked his head. "Come here, pretty lady."

Georgia pressed her face against his chest as he wrapped her in his embrace and kissed the top of her head.

She clung to him, pressed her lips to his with a desperation that made him weak and wanting more. His resolve to be a gentleman was vanishing.

With all the strength he could muster, Romel finished the kiss and laid his forehead on hers. Studied her eyes. She whispered, "I don't want you to leave."

"If I don't, we'll do something we might regret."

She squeezed her eyes closed, inhaled through her teeth, and blew it out. "You might be right, but I'm not sure I care."

"Then let's wait until you *are* sure. I want you to be sure."

She nodded, blew another burst of air through her teeth. Offered a smile. "Come back for breakfast?"

He bobbed his head. The corners of his mouth curled up. He was already counting the hours until he'd see her again.

CHAPTER EIGHT

GEORGIA STOOD IN THE doorway and watched Romel pull out of her driveway. She laid her palms over her burning cheeks, then touched her fingertips to her mouth, already yearning for Romel's lips.

In her room, Georgia studied her reflection in the full-length mirror. She was such a dirty mess, yet Romel had held her and kissed her. Her lips curled into a knowing smile. She wanted more than someone to eat supper with. She wanted more than a companion—needed more than a companion. She wanted a relationship with Romel.

After her shower, Georgia climbed into her bed and turned on the bedside lamp. She ran her fingers over the photo of William. "I will always love you, my darling. But I'm lonely, and I don't want to turn out like Harriet—alone and cantankerous and expecting our daughter to fill in the lonesome hours." She waited, as if William would give her a sign. "I couldn't save you and I'm frightened I can't take care of any living thing. But I need to try. I have to trust I can build a relationship with Romel."

She kissed his photo, then stashed it away in a drawer.

It was before eight in the morning when Georgia strolled into her garden without William's journal. She no longer felt the need to record everything. That was William's process. She'd hire a gardener to take care of the pests, the fertilizing, and the pruning. Her time was better spent with Romel and the animals at the shelter. She picked four oranges to squeeze for juice, enough for two glasses, and smiled. William so loved this garden. He would want her to enjoy the fruit, and she knew now that he wouldn't want her to be alone. She bobbed her head. Despite their differences, William and Romel had a lot in common. They were both loving, gentle, and romantic. They would have liked one another.

She joined her new man in the kitchen. Romel kissed her cheek. "Good morning, pretty lady."

She made juice and coffee, and he cooked omelets. They worked well together, sashaying around one another, enjoying simple tasks in the kitchen.

"You might need to take over more of the cooking." Georgia wiggled her eyebrows. "This is the best omelet I've ever tasted."

"I can do that. I like to cook." He gave her that cocky grin. The one that made her knees go weak. "I'd especially like to make you breakfast more often. I enjoy starting my day with you."

"I think we can arrange that."

"Good, because I make a pretty good macadamia nut waffle."

She shook her head. "That does it. You are now the chief cook."

Romel smiled over the rim of his coffee cup. "How about I bring Bert back with me around five?"

"That's fine. How about grilled chicken and a green salad for supper?"

"No pie?"

"Not unless you've got one stashed over at your place."

He rubbed his chin, narrowed his eyes conspiratorially. "It takes less than an hour to whip up a graham cracker crust banana cream pie. I harvested some bananas from my yard a couple of days ago. They're begging to be eaten."

"Sounds delicious, but we better make some rules around how many times a week I eat pie." She laughed and patted her tummy. "I don't want to add any more pounds to this body."

His face turned serious. He reached across the table and took her hand. "You would still be perfect."

Perfect? She lowered her gaze and covered her grin with her hand.

Georgia walked him to the door. He wrapped his arms around her and trailed kisses from her mouth to her ear. "I love you, pretty lady."

Three years of emptiness vanished. Her heart was bursting. She pulled him closer. "I love you too. More than you know."

She pressed her mouth to his and savored his taste, the feel of his lips, the promise they held. He stepped away, blew out a big puff of air. "You really get me going. If I don't leave right now, I'm afraid I'll get carried away."

She threw her head back and laughed. "Then you better get going."

He grasped her hands, gazed into her eyes. "I'm one lucky guy. I can't wait for my kids to meet you. They're gonna love you as much as I do."

Before going to the grocery store, Georgia popped in at the shelter to see how Onyx was doing. She found Dr. Dave in the classroom. He reported, "He's improving but would benefit from more human contact. My interns are pretty tied up caring for the Dobie pups. Turns out the pups are a great learning experience for them."

"May I take him to the play yard?"

"That'd be great." He headed out the door, then stopped and turned to face her. "He misses you. And for the record, you are not responsible for his condition or the seizure."

"Thank you. I miss him too."

She sprinted to Onyx's kennel, opened the latch, and kneeled to hug him. He reciprocated by licking her face and moving his backend so rapidly, they both fell to the floor in a heap.

"Your boyfriend isn't enough?" Harriet stood over them *tsk-tsking* and wagging her finger. "You have to roll around with a dog too?"

The hair on the back of Georgia's neck tingled. Of all the volunteers to observe her on the floor, it had to be Harriet. "A boyfriend? I know you'd like me to have a boyfriend, but where did you get the idea that I have one?"

Harriet shook her finger in Georgia's face. "Shame on you. Having that painter spend the night at your house for all your neighbors to see."

"He didn't spend the night."

"Then why was his truck parked in your drive all night? Jennifer said she saw his truck when she went to stay at her sister's house last night *and* it was still there this morning."

"Oh, that." Jennifer. She should have known. She didn't owe Harriet any explanation at all, but she sure didn't want rumors spread about her and Romel. They hadn't even met one another's kids or discussed what that meant to their relationship. She pasted on a smile. "Even though it is nobody's business, please inform Jennifer that I hired Romel—Mr. Bautista—to clean up my aviary and then he came again this morning to deliver some materials for the project."

The part about hiring him was an outright lie, and the last part of her explanation was misleading, but darn it, Georgia wasn't ready for people to know they shared breakfast together.

"*Humph*! I don't believe a word of it. And another thing, if that painter is such a great catch, why doesn't he drive a nicer truck? Why, if my husband were still alive, he'd sell him a newer model."

"I'm sure he would, Harriet. Your husband was a shrewd salesman and a good man. I know it must be difficult for you to live alone. I'm sure you miss him."

Harriet swiped a tear from her cheek and pulled her shoulders back. "I'm quite capable of taking care of myself."

"Of course you are."

The old woman ambled away, loneliness frothing in her wake.

Georgia knew all about loneliness and what it could do to a person. Or to an animal. Her future would not look like Harriet's! She clipped a leash on Onyx and walked to Lani's office to fill out adoption papers.

Romel got the text ten minutes before he arrived at Georgia's: *Park in the garage.*

He didn't know why, but he was sure she had her reasons.

The garage door was open, so he pulled in. Georgia lowered the door before he could even get out of his vehicle. "What's up?"

"Just trying to protect our privacy. One of the interns at the shelter saw your truck parked in my drive last night and again this morning and made some assumptions." Dragging her hands through her hair, Georgia let out an exasperated sigh. "She felt a need to report that to others at the shelter, including Harriet."

He wrapped his arms around her. "Does it matter if people know we're more than friends?"

"It matters to me. I think we should tell our kids first. Make sure they're all on board with our relationship. Don't you think?"

"I'm ready to be more open, but our kids get here soon so, if that's what makes you the most comfortable, that's what we'll do."

Georgia smiled. "Okay, we'll stay away from each other at the shelter. And when you come for supper, you should park in the garage. We can handle that, right?"

"Like I said, if that's what you want, then that's what we'll do." He shifted his stance, not at all sure if it was okay to kiss her.

She wrapped her arms around his neck. "It's only a few more days until our kids arrive and you host the barbeque for the shelter volunteers. I promise if we get a green light from our kids, I'll kiss you in front of everyone there."

"Do I have to wait for that kiss?"

Georgia leaned into him and gazed into his eyes. "Not on my account."

The kiss was a perfect reminder of why Romel wanted Georgia in his life. Difficult as it was to stop kissing her, he stepped away. "Anyway, thanks for taking Bert this week so I have time to clean thoroughly before Tommy brings his gal to the house." He unloaded Bert's cage from the passenger side of his truck. As soon as Bert saw Georgia, he called, "Kiss her quick." Romel grinned and happily obliged.

"Evening, Bert." Georgia clicked her tongue at him. "Shall we get him settled in the aviary? I have something to show you."

"Well, let's get going then." He followed her into the mudroom and was met by a Rottweiler.

"I adopted him today. This is Onyx." She rubbed his head and beamed.

"What changed your mind about having a pet in the house?"

"It was a combination of things people said—you, Dr. Dave, and surprisingly, Harriet. I decided Onyx deserved to live out his years with a companion."

He set down Bert's cage. His voice hitched. "We all deserve that."

Georgia rested her head on his shoulder. Romel breathed in the scent of lavender before he settled his lips squarely on her mouth. "Now that I've found you, I don't know what I'd do without you."

"Bake more pies?" She wiggled her eyebrows.

The next day, Romel waved to Georgia from his perch on the manlift. She bowed her head and hurried into the shelter. He'd be glad when this nonsense of pretending was finished. But he'd agreed to wait until their kids arrived and gave their blessing before they let on about their relationship. That day couldn't come fast enough.

He contemplated holding her at suppertime and sharing some kisses and making plans for their future together. His house or hers? Did he care?

His phone buzzed. Princess. "Hi, honey."

"Hi, Daddy. I have a surprise for you. I'm bringing someone home with me."

"You are?"

"I am, but I'm not going to tell you who it is until I get there."

"Turns out, I have a surprise for you too." He chuckled. "And I'm not going to tell *you* until you get here."

"You're not selling our house, are you?"

"No. I'm not selling the house."

"Oh good. I love our house. Anyway, Daddy, class is starting. We'll catch a cab from the airport, so you don't have to leave the barbeque to pick us up."

"Can't wait to see you and to meet your friend. Love you."

"Love you too. Bye."

He shook his head and smiled. Princess had always loved surprises. Loved being surprised and loved surprising others. He wondered whether she was bringing home a boy.

Romel resumed painting the eaves a shade of blue darker than the walls. He wouldn't get back to painting until after his kids' visit. He was a little behind schedule but hoped to make it up after the holiday weekend. And once the holiday weekend was over, Georgia would acknowledge their relationship to the other volunteers, and he could once again eat his lunch with her in the break room. As it was, he'd asked her to eat at a different time because being in the same room without gazing at her was dang near impossible. At least she'd agreed to eat supper with him every evening, so he had that to look forward to.

At precisely ten of six, Romel pulled into Georgia's garage and closed the door behind him with the remote garage door opener she'd given him. Onyx met him at the doorway, bouncing on his paws, begging for a pat. Romel couldn't resist and rolled around on the floor with him until Georgia entered the room and Onyx's attention shifted to her.

Romel stood and planted a kiss on Georgia's cheek. "Let's get to our supper and then make some plans for our kids to get together when they're here."

"I thought that's why you're hosting the barbeque their first night in," Georgia said.

"Partly. I was thinking to start with a big group, then have something like a game night with just us." He gazed at her. "You know, like one family."

Her face lit up. "One family. I'd like that."

Chapter Nine

Georgia waited near the baggage claim at the Hilo International Airport. She glanced at her watch for the umpteenth time since learning Samantha and Jim's flight would be over an hour late. Her knee bounced on the wooden bench—each little jolt a reminder that continuing her relationship with Romel would be decided today. They'd agreed that their kids needed to be comfortable with their relationship. At Christmas time, when Samantha and Jim visited, it seemed that Samantha missed her dad a lot. She was almost in a state of depression—unusual for her jolly self. Georgia sure didn't want to send her daughter into a tailspin. Her priority was her daughter's happiness.

The sight of Samantha and Jim waving from the throng of arriving travelers dissolved her anxiety. She wrapped her arms around her daughter and rocked her back and forth.

"Wow, Mom. You look different than you did at Christmas time." Samantha studied Georgia's face. "Are you taking some new supplements or something? You're simply glowing."

Georgia felt the heat rush to her cheeks. "Thank you. I'm just so happy you two are here."

Jim embraced her and kissed her cheek. "And we're happy to be out of the Iowa heat and humidity."

"I hope you feel up to the barbeque for the shelter volunteers."

"We do, right, Jim?"

"Right." Jim grabbed their luggage from the carousel. "Ready."

"Let's stop by the house first so you can freshen up." Georgia grinned. "I have a little surprise."

Onyx met them at the door. "Oh my gosh!" Samantha kneeled to cuddle the dog. "What's his name?"

"Onyx. I adopted him. Isn't he marvelous?"

Jim joined Samantha on the floor. "How great you have him to keep you company in this big house."

Heat climbed up Georgia's face. Wait till you see who else keeps me company, she thought.

As soon as they got to the barbeque, Georgia led her family across the lawn to meet Romel. After introductions, Samantha sent Jim for cold drinks, looped her arm through Georgia's and whispered, "How serious is it?"

Georgia blushed. "Is it that obvious? Are you okay with me dating?"

"Okay? Mom, it's great!" Samantha hugged her and swayed back and forth.

Jim handed them each a cold drink. "Looks like we're all happy here."

"I figured out what that glow is on Mom's face. She's in love."

Jim held a pretend microphone to Georgia's mouth. "Can you confirm the allegation that you are in love?"

"Maybe not love. Not yet." She bit her lips and felt the flush of heat that seemed to creep up her face at the mention of Romel. "We are dating, though."

"And who is this lucky man?" He continued the fake interview.

"Our host." Samantha squealed before she hugged Georgia again. "I can't believe you didn't tell us!"

"So, you're not upset? You don't think it's too soon?"

Samantha held both her hands. "Mom, Dad's been gone for three years. I'm thrilled you've moved on."

Georgia waited until Samantha was engaged in conversation with Auntie Lei to approach Romel at the grill. "We've been outed."

His grin spread across his face like wildfire. "Can I kiss you then?"

"Later. We haven't heard the verdict from your kids."

"Well, it just so happens that I already told Tommy about you, and he said if it made me happy, then he's happy for us."

She turned her head toward his ear. "As soon as your youngest gets here and we see she feels the same, I promise to kiss you smack on your lips in front of everyone."

Romel craned his neck. "It won't be long now. Princess just arrived." He smiled and waved. Someone else stepped from the cab. What the devil was going on? Cynthia?

He dropped his hand to his side. Georgia touched his arm. "Who's that with your daughter?"

His tongue swelled in his mouth. "My ex-wife."

Georgia removed her hand and stepped back.

"Wait." His jaw tightened and body tensed.

Cynthia wrapped her arms around him and kissed him squarely on the mouth. "Princess tells me you want me back"—she licked her lips—"so here I am."

He jerked away. Spun around and saw Georgia racing toward the street, fists at her sides, her family in tow.

Teeth clenched, he took Cynthia's arm and marched her into the house.

"What the hell are you doing? You can't just waltz in here and expect me to welcome you back into my life."

She laid her palm on his chest. "I told you, Princess said you wanted me back." She gazed at him, tilted her head. "I'm sorry if I caught you off guard. I thought it would be a welcomed surprise."

"You thought wrong."

"At any rate, I wanted to see Tommy and meet Dana. You wouldn't deny me that, would you?"

"No. Of course not. It's just that—"

"There you two are," Princess said from the doorway. "You can talk more later. C'mon Mama, Tommy wants to introduce you to Dana."

Romel had guests. He had burgers to cook. He would straighten this out later, after Georgia cooled down.

Georgia's heart pounded in her ears. "I need to get out of here."

She shoved the car keys into Jim's hand, dropped into the back seat, and folded her arms across her chest. Was she angrier at Romel for not being open about his feelings for Cynthia or with herself for falling in love with him?

"Mom?" Samantha slid in beside her. "What happened? I thought things were going great and now—well, now you look furious."

Georgia clenched her jaw. She *was* furious for falling for him, for craving more than a companion. "His ex-wife showed up."

Samantha patted Georgia's arm. "Maybe she always comes to family celebrations. Maybe they have an understanding."

"She kissed him right on the mouth. Evidently, Romel sent a message through their daughter that he wanted her back. I feel so stupid. Like a placeholder until Cynthia made up her mind." She stared out the window. "I guess he has his answer."

"Did he know she was coming?"

Georgia mopped sweat from her brow. "Does it matter?"

"Of course it matters," Jim said. "What if he's just as surprised as you? When my parents divorced, I wanted them to get back together more than anything. And I tried lots of crazy ploys to make that happen. Maybe his daughter is doing the same thing."

Samantha squeezed Georgia's hand. "Jim's right. At least give him a chance to explain."

"It seems pretty clear to me what happened. He was just waiting for her to come back, and she did."

The two-mile drive lasted an eternity. Romel once said he would have given anything to keep his family together. If Georgia had paid attention to all his words, not just the ones that boosted her ego, she wouldn't be in this situation. She desperately needed to take a long shower and wash away any thoughts of Romel and the life she thought they were building together.

As soon as Jim parked the car, Georgia leaped out and slammed the door.

"Mom." Samantha grasped her shoulders. "You're scaring me. I've never seen you this angry."

Despite her raw nerves, Georgia forced herself to calm down. The last thing she wanted was to upset her daughter. "I'm sorry. I'll be fine." She waved her hand and shrugged. "I just need to get some rest. You two must be starved. Take the car and go get something to eat, okay?"

They entered the mudroom. Onyx licked their hands and danced at their feet.

"Are you sure you'll be all right?" Samantha frowned, her words laced with concern.

Georgia forced a smile. "I'm sure. Go on now." She kissed Samantha on the cheek. "See you in the morning. I need to be at the festival to organize the food booth by eight."

"Maybe we'll take Onyx for a walk on the beach. Would that be okay?"

"He'd like that."

Georgia reached down and scrubbed her fingers across Onyx's back. Adopting him had been the best decision she'd made since William died. At least Onyx would keep her company once the kids flew home.

Romel's ringtone taunted her. Georgia threw the phone on the bed and stomped to the bathroom. She wasn't ready to hear his voice, wasn't sure she could stand to hear him apologize for wanting his family reunited.

Georgia set the shower head to the highest pressure and stood beneath the hot, pounding water. She rolled her neck and shoulders, inhaled the steamy air, and massaged her temples to let go of her fury at herself for being so naïve. She never expected it to hurt this much.

Turning her face to the spray, she closed her eyes and saw only Romel—in her kitchen, in the aviary, grilling in her backyard. The recollections enveloped her and diluted her anger. How could he be the two-timer she'd conjured when Cynthia kissed him?

What if Jim was right? What if Princess had orchestrated her parents' reunion without Romel's knowledge? What if Cynthia was the pawn? Georgia's throat constricted. She'd allowed jealousy to rule her and fled rather than giving Romel a chance to explain.

Ever since she'd struggled to dial 9-1-1 when William collapsed on their evening walk, she'd been incapable of handling emotional strain. Her nursing instincts to act quickly had been reprogrammed to flight or freeze responses. How would she ever be able to commit to someone if she continued to respond like that?

She stepped from the shower and rubbed the water from her body while loneliness seeped into every pore. She already missed Romel.

CHAPTER TEN

PRINCESS AND CYNTHIA STOOD at the grill, flipping burgers and hot dogs, and chatting away like nothing was wrong. Romel took the spatula from Cynthia. "I'll get this. Go eat. We'll talk later."

After Cynthia walked away, Princess bounced on her toes, eyes wide. "Well? Are you surprised?"

"What were you thinking, bringing your mama here without telling me?"

She pushed out her bottom lip and looped her arm through his. "We've been talking and she's lonely, Daddy. And you're lonely too. I can tell. And since neither of you is seeing anyone—"

"That's just it. I have been seeing someone and now she's left the party because of your shenanigans. I planned to introduce you."

"Well, I don't think I want to meet her. You and Mama already know each other. It just makes sense that you get back together."

Romel searched his daughter's eyes for understanding. "If we were meant to be together, we'd still be together."

"You'll see, Daddy." Princess laid her head against his shoulder. "Mama changed her mind. She wants to come home."

She ran off to join Cynthia, Tommy, and Dana.

He couldn't wait any longer. Romel slipped into the house and dialed Georgia's cell. She didn't pick up, and he didn't leave a message. Voicemail could not record all he needed to say.

Lani cornered him on his back lanai. "Is Georgia okay? She left before I even got a chance to say hi. I can't reach her on her cell."

Romel licked his lips and hung his head. "We had a misunderstanding. She left early."

"Oh. I'm sorry."

"I'm sure we'll get it sorted out."

"Get what sorted out?" Harriet's voice came from behind him. "Is there some problem with the schedule for the food booth? I knew this thing wouldn't go smoothly with Georgia in charge."

"There's no problem with the schedule, Mother. Everything is just fine."

"Then what needs sorting out?"

Lani took Harriet's arm. "It's not our concern."

"Are we going to stay here all night?" Harriet scrunched her brows. "We have to work at the festival tomorrow, you know."

"You're right. We'll go now. Mahalo, Romel. We'll see you tomorrow."

By the time the rest of the guests left, Romel had tried Georgia's cell seven times. After the clean-up, Princess set up the Monopoly board on the kitchen table while Tommy poured cold drinks for everyone. "C'mon, Daddy. Sit by Mama. I gave you the cannon token, just like always."

Romel could have chosen the tokens for his family—the ship for Tommy, the Scottie dog for Cynthia, and the race car for Princess. After Dana chose the shoe, Princess announced, "That will be your token all the time now. We play with the same ones every time."

"That's right." Cynthia held the Scottie dog to her cheek. "My family always lets me have this little guy."

Tommy joined in. "You can keep your dog, Mama. My ship is sailing for a win."

"Not if my car races to the finish first." Princess drove the car around the board.

The predictability of his family's boasts calmed Romel. He'd planned to drive to Georgia's and pound on the door until she talked to him, but the expectation on the faces of his family convinced him to stay put.

Tommy cheered when Dana won, and Princess gathered them for a group selfie. She informed them she was going to order copies for everyone, so they'd all have a family photo with Dana in it.

Cynthia yawned. "This was fun, but I can't keep my eyes open any longer."

Tommy challenged them to another game, and tempting as it was to spend more time with his kids, Romel said he was beat and went to his room to try Georgia's cell again. "C'mon, Georgia. Pick up."

All he got was voicemail. Again. And he wasn't about to leave a message about how he needed to talk to her. He slammed the phone into his back pocket. He didn't want to explain to his kids where he was going, but they were still playing a game in the kitchen. Feeling like a louse, but determined to leave without being questioned, Romel left through the sliding glass door to the master bedroom. His kids would hear the garage door open and the truck start up, but he was going anyway.

Georgia had to talk to him. She'd want him to come after her. That was a sign that he was in the wrong, wasn't it? What if the lights were out? He'd ring the doorbell only if the lights were on.

He gripped the steering wheel until his knuckles throbbed. The lights in Georgia's living room were on. Romel would explain that he did not invite Cynthia and beg Georgia's forgiveness.

Samantha answered the door. Romel peeked around her. "I'd like to speak to your mama."

"She's resting."

"Is there any way you could get her to come talk to me? I need to explain something to her." He dragged his fingers across his scalp and squeezed the back of his neck.

"Look, Romel, Mom isn't ready to talk to you." Her tone was apologetic. "Give her time and I'm sure she'll listen."

"Would you give her a message for me?"

"Sure."

"Tell her I didn't invite Cynthia."

Romel stared at his feet and blinked back the moisture from his eyes. Samantha touched his arm. "I'll tell her."

She smiled a tentative kind of smile and closed the door. Romel leaned against the house and allowed a single tear to escape. He couldn't lose Georgia. He'd do whatever it took to get things back the way they were.

By daybreak, of all the emotions that clung to Georgia, loneliness prevailed. She was ready to talk to Romel in person. She needed to see his face and give him a chance to explain. And after she listened, she'd ask for his patience while she worked through her urge to flee when things got tough.

Georgia took Onyx for a walk, spent some time with Bert, and picked three oranges for breakfast. Samantha and Jim joined her in the sunroom, mugs of coffee in their hands, and worried looks on their faces.

"Good morning." Georgia offered a genuine smile. "Sorry about last night."

Samantha curled up on a settee. "You seem better."

"I am. I just needed to think it through. I overreacted. I'll take Jim's advice and talk to Romel today. Did you find something good to eat last night?"

"We had papaya with two scoops of macadamia nut ice cream."

Georgia raised her eyebrows. "That's all you ate?"

Jim shrugged. "It was delicious."

"Tonight, I'm going to cook Samantha's favorite, so don't fill up at the festival."

"Grilled ahi," Samantha and Jim said in unison.

Georgia slapped her hands on the table and stood up. "If you take me to the fairgrounds, then you can have the car today."

After Samantha dropped her off, Georgia reworked the assignments so that she and Romel would be as far from one another as possible in the twelve-by-eight-foot booth space until they could manage a mutual break and talk. She'd prep the salad-on-a-stick, and he'd cook the sausage kabobs.

Lani and Harriet arrived before Romel to help set up. Lani pulled Georgia into the parking lot away from the others. "Are you okay? Romel said you two had a misunderstanding."

"I feel so foolish." She closed her eyes and wrapped her arms in front of her chest. "His ex-wife showed up. She kissed him on the lips and said their daughter told her Romel wanted her back. When I heard that, I freaked. Like always."

"I met Cynthia. If it makes you feel any better, Romel seemed to avoid her at the barbeque. She mostly visited with their kids."

"I refused to answer his calls. I had to think through it. I'm afraid I've made a bad situation worse by ignoring him."

"Anything I can do to help?"

"I'll let you know. My plan is to schedule us for a break at the same time and have a private conversation." She twisted the hemline of her shirt. "I don't want to lose him, but I'm not sure I can promise any man I'll be able to keep it together when things get tough."

Lani rubbed her back. "I'm here if you need me."

"Lani?" Harriet's stony voice skittered across the parking lot.

Georgia and Lani looked at each other, shook their heads, and headed back toward the booth.

"Sounds like you might be the one who needs help." Georgia wrapped her arm around Lani's waist and hugged her.

The savory smell of peppers, onions, and sausage wafted from the booth. Romel nodded at her but said nothing. She nearly forgot he was working behind her until his family approached.

"Daddy, smile while I get a picture of you working." Princess positioned her phone. "Now Mama, stand by the booth so I can get a picture of the two of you."

Cynthia looked triumphant when she leaned across the counter and tilted her head toward Romel. Princess stood right in front of Georgia and gestured for her to move. Georgia wiped her hands on her apron and mumbled an excuse while she slunk away, but not before Princess bellowed, "Guess what, Daddy? Mama can stay with us at your house for two more nights. Isn't that great?"

Harriet turned her head away from the cash box and clucked her tongue.

Georgia fled and ducked into the women's restroom. She rinsed her face with cold water to wash away the images that percolated in her mind. Had Romel slept with Cynthia? Is that why she looked at him so adoringly? Like a spy, Georgia peeked around the doorway and was relieved to see that Romel's family had walked on down the lane. She smoothed her apron and marched toward the food booth. A hand on her shoulder stopped her.

"Georgia. Wait. Please."

She turned to face Romel's steel-gray eyes.

"Let me explain."

She gulped down her doubts. "I'm ready to listen."

"Princess has this insane idea that her mama and I should get back together, but that's not at all what I want."

She bit her lip. Stepped closer. "What *do* you want, Romel?"

He backed up. "I want us"—he scanned the area with nervous eyes and squeezed the back of his neck—"it's just that I'll have to keep my distance while Princess is in town. She needs time to understand that her mama and I are not meant for each other. I can't alienate my daughter more than I already have. Not after the trauma of the divorce." He held Georgia's gaze, his eyes begging. "I promised myself when my kids were born that they'd be my priority. I know what it's like to have parents who disregard their kids. My parents were pretty absent when I was growing up."

Georgia stepped back. Reconciliation dissolving like cotton candy in a rainstorm. "I see. And will Cynthia be staying with you in the meantime?"

"There are no hotel rooms available for the weekend. And she's bunking with Princess, not me, in case that's what you're thinking. I'll get her out of the house as soon as a hotel room is available."

Georgia bit her lip. "I don't think I care when she leaves. We agreed that our kids had to be okay with our relationship, and obviously that's not the case. You can't deny that Princess might never accept me. I'll walk away now, and you can make peace with your daughter."

She turned on her heels, struggled to keep upright. It was preposterous she'd thought she could have a relationship with another man. She beelined to the parking lot. Held back her tears until she was sure no one could see her.

CHAPTER ELEVEN

ROMEL'S HEAD THROBBED. He wanted Georgia in his life, and he wanted Princess to like her. It looked like both were out of his control.

He gazed at the line forming at the food booth and massaged the back of his neck. He returned to what he could control—cooking up skewers of sausage and peppers.

How could he work this close to Georgia for another two days? Yes, they agreed they wanted their kids to be comfortable with the relationship, but it never occurred to him that his daughter might be the one to sabotage their plans. If only Princess could spend some time with Georgia, she'd see how wonderful she was.

"Romel?" Harriet demanded. "Order up. Do you need another break? You can't cook and stare into space at the same time."

He shook himself and forced a smile. "Sorry. I'm on it."

During the next lull, Tommy approached the booth and asked Georgia when he might go see Bert. She said she'd call Samantha and let her know he was coming if he wanted to go now. Princess sidled up to Tommy. "Mama and I wanna see Bert too."

Romel spoke up, louder than he'd planned. "I don't think that's a good idea, Princess."

"But I haven't seen Bert since Easter weekend." Princess pouted and cocked her head.

The other volunteers stopped what they were doing and looked at their feet. "Why don't you just go with your brother and have your mama go back to the house with Dana?"

"Come on, Daddy. Please. Mama wants to see Bert too."

He shuffled his feet and screwed up his mouth. What would it hurt for Cynthia to go see Bert?

"Oh, all right. I'm sure Georgia won't mind."

Georgia spun around and glared at him, then squeezed her eyes shut and mustered her last ounce of civility. "You go ahead, Princess and Cynthia. You should all go see Bert."

"You two are something else." Harriet snickered. "Can't you save your spat for another time when we don't all have to listen?"

Harriet was right. Heat spread across Georgia's cheeks. "I'll call Samantha right now." She walked away from the booth and punched in the number. "Are you still at the house?"

"No, we're taking Onyx for a walk on the beach before we come to the festival. Why?"

Georgia refused to disrupt her own daughter's plans to accommodate Romel's spoiled brat. "Just checking. Have a good walk. I'll see you later."

She didn't want to think about it all day. Somehow, Georgia had to figure out how to unlock the house for Romel's family to see Bert. She could give Tommy the key to her house and risk Princess and Cynthia snooping in places they didn't belong, or ask Romel to take them, but he was the chief cook for the food booth, or she could take them herself.

Her jaw tightened as she walked away from the booth. Romel's family was waiting for an answer.

"I have a suggestion." Lani's voice sliced through her frustration. "Unlike your shift, ours is almost over. I'll drive Mother home and come back to finish your duties." She hugged Georgia. "Honestly, you're in no shape to be managing the booth today. You can take my car."

Georgia allowed the growl she'd buried in her throat to escape. "Did you see the way he gives in to that whiney daughter of his?"

"How old is she?"

"Eighteen. And her name is Princess. And the whole family treats her as if she were royalty. There's no way I want to compete with that."

Lani's tone changed. "I don't blame you. I wouldn't want to come between a dad and his daughter either"—she gritted her teeth—"like my mother did."

It was Georgia's turn to hug Lani. "Your mother is right about one thing. Romel and I need to keep our spat private."

They walked back to the booth arm in arm; Georgia's resolve to get this over with increased with each step.

Hands clasped in front of her, Georgia pasted on a smile. She narrowed her eyes to block out Princess as she approached

Romel's family. "I'll take you to see Bert as soon as Lani drives her mother home and returns to cover my duties. Meet me back here in thirty minutes."

"Thank you," Cynthia offered. "This means a lot to me. Bert's been part of our family for a long time."

Georgia softened her tone. "You're welcome."

Romel's family strolled away, as carefree as butterflies in the breeze. Georgia slapped on a pair of plastic gloves and busied herself with prepping the caprese salad-on-a-stick. Romel sidled up next to her. "I hope you don't mind Cynthia going along. Bert is like a third child to us."

She lifted a skewer, stabbed it through a tomato, and pierced the fruit into a pulp.

Lani handed her car keys to Georgia. "Keep strong, sweetie."

Romel's family met her at the booth. Before they got to the parking lot, Princess called shotgun and jumped into the front passenger's seat the moment Georgia unlocked the car. Thank goodness the ride was short. Princess turned up the volume on the radio and sang. Tommy and Cynthia joined in the sing-along. Cynthia's delight didn't escape Georgia. She couldn't fault a woman who enjoyed being with her kids. When the song was done, Cynthia asked Princess to lower the volume, then said, "Thanks for housing Bert so Dana could stay at the house."

"I'm happy to." Georgia meant that. Bert was much easier to deal with than most people she knew.

Georgia opened the front door and invited them in. Princess stopped in the foyer. "Wow. This looks like a house for movie stars. Can we see the rest?"

Cynthia took her daughter's arm. "We're here to see Bert. We won't impose on Georgia more than that."

"He's in there." Georgia opened the door to the den and led them to the aviary.

Bert squawked and flapped his wings. He flew to Cynthia, landed on her shoulder, and nuzzled her cheek. Princess beamed. "Ah, Mama, he remembers you."

The scene reminded Georgia of her college days when she'd reunite with her dog during school breaks. Pets do become members of the family. She'd done the right thing by agreeing to Cynthia's visit with Bert. Cynthia wasn't the enemy. She was a woman trying to spend time with her family. And Georgia could see now that Princess just wanted her family together like it used to be. Georgia knew what it was to miss the way one's family used to be. She left them alone for their reunion. It was the right decision to walk away from Romel and not complicate their family dynamics.

If only her heart believed that were true.

Romel sat on his lanai with his head in his hands. He wanted Georgia, and he wanted to maintain a good relationship with his daughter. How to juggle that was a complete mystery to him.

Cynthia joined him on the porch swing, so close their thighs touched.

"Cynthia, I don't know what you're trying to do here."

"I think you do." She wrapped her arms around his neck.

Romel slid away from her. "You know I never told Princess I wanted to get back together."

She narrowed her eyebrows. "But we could do fine, don't you think? We know all the things to avoid."

"We can get along, if that's what you mean."

"I'm more interested in getting back together as a family. Even though the kids are grown, I like the feeling of us all being in the same house, playing games and joking around. I'm ready to try again, Romel."

"Listen. I don't know where Princess got the idea that I wanted you to come back. You and I tried to make our relationship work, and we divorced. End of story."

Cynthia squeezed his knee. "Aren't you lonely?"

"I was, but not anymore." He pushed her hand away. "I'm sorry you were under the false assumption that I wanted you back. I don't wish anything bad for you, Cynthia, but I don't want to try again. I've moved on and so should you."

"Truth time?"

"Sure."

"Is it Georgia?"

"Yes."

"She seems nice enough. A little jittery, but otherwise—"

"She's jittery, as you put it, because we thought her daughter would like me and that our kids would like her. And since Princess is hell-bent on my getting back together with you, she can't see past that and won't give Georgia a chance."

"I had no idea you were in a committed relationship."

"Well, I thought I was until this whole mess with Princess. Georgia broke it off today."

"I'm sorry. Can I be honest with you?"

"That's always best."

"When Princess said you wanted me back, I thought it was worth a try. I figured it was better than being alone because I haven't found anyone else. But I hope you and Georgia get things worked out."

Romel scratched his chin. "Would you tell Princess that? Help me convince her to give Georgia a chance?"

"Yeah, I'll tell her. I don't know whether she'll listen. Our Princess is immature in a lot of ways. And she's stubborn."

"I wonder where she gets that from?"

Cynthia smacked him on the arm. "You might as well cancel the hotel room. I'll make reservations to fly home on Monday, and I'll take Princess with me. She needs to return to school, anyway."

On the way to the airport, Georgia blinked back the familiar tears that came with saying goodbye to Samantha. Her brave face dissolved with their final hug. "I already miss you."

Samantha kissed her cheek. "At least you have Onyx for company. And Mom, don't give up on Romel. Things might still work out."

Jim took Samantha's hand, and they disappeared into the throng of people waiting in the TSA line.

It was just like Samantha to think positively. Georgia fumbled with her car keys, dropped them on the hot pavement, and stared at her keychain. Believe. One word on the little metal disc. Did she dare believe Samantha was right? Believe that things might still work out with Romel?

Relieved the day would be busy, she drove straight to the animal shelter to reconcile the accounting for the fundraiser before her noon meeting with Lani. She stepped from her car and immediately scanned the area for any sign of Romel. It would be easier if she didn't have to see him, but she still had Bert in her aviary, so they'd have to see one another for that exchange.

After Georgia gave a chunk of broccoli to Franklin and dropped a handful of sunflower seeds into Trudy's tray, she went to the break room to get a cup of coffee. The three interns at the table stopped talking. She knew the gossip about her and Romel was rampant, fodder as good as a soap opera. She held her head high and nodded her greeting to the group, then slipped out and cursed under her breath for getting herself into a situation where she was the subject of gossip.

By the time Lani arrived for their meeting, Georgia's embarrassment had festered for almost an hour. Her head shot up. "What are they saying about me?"

Lani screwed up her mouth. "Hello to you too."

"I'm sorry." Georgia hunched her shoulders and shook her head. "I just don't like people speculating about my private life. It's humiliating."

"You know the coconut wireless. Some say you had a big fight in the middle of the fairgrounds and others say Romel flaunted his ex-wife after leading you on."

"What does your mother say?" Georgia blurted, then lowered her chin. "I'm sorry Lani. That was uncalled for."

"It's okay. It's the truth. Mother is a gossip." Lani shrugged and let out a little chortle. "I'm the one who should apologize. Mother seems to have it out for you."

"She does, but I know *you* don't feel that way. I try to ignore her comments although it's increasingly more difficult."

"If it makes you feel any better, I thought you and Romel were great together. He seems so sweet."

"He is ... was ... sweet. I don't even know now. And he didn't flaunt his ex." Tears cascaded down her cheeks. "We are good together, but his daughter doesn't want me around."

Lani tipped her chin toward the door and raised her eyebrows.

Georgia quickly swiped her face with a tissue and turned. Romel stood in the doorway, his hat clutched in his hands, and shoulders drooping. "I wondered if it'd be okay to pick up Bert later?"

She clasped her trembling hands in her lap. "What time?"

"Whatever suits you."

"Five then. I'll have Bert's things gathered up."

He nodded, a grin blooming, and retreated without another word.

"Did you see that?" Fresh tears stung Georgia's cheeks. "Did you see that grin? He's happy to be done with me."

CHAPTER TWELVE

SHE'D BEEN CRYING. AND as much as Romel hated to see her upset, those tears had made him smile, given him hope that they still had a chance, if only Georgia would give Princess time to come around.

At exactly five o'clock, he stood at Georgia's front door with a bouquet of heart-shaped anthuriums so large it covered his chest.

"Can we talk?" Romel pushed the bouquet forward. Her hands dropped to her sides. He frowned and set the flowers on the side table.

She crossed her arms in front of her chest. "I don't think there's anything else to say."

"Princess and Cynthia left this morning. I thought we could plan a supper to talk about how to handle our situation."

"Our situation is handled." Her chin quivered, and she looked away.

Romel reached for her. She stumbled backward. "I won't compete with your daughter, and I don't expect you to choose between us. We're better off just forgetting we ever had suppers together."

"It'd be easier to forget if I didn't think about you every dang minute." He grabbed her hand. "And we had more than suppers together. I thought we had something special. Please, just say you'll give Princess time to get used to the idea of us."

"How long?" Her shoulders shook, and she didn't even bother to wipe her tears. "It doesn't look like Princess will change her mind, and I can't live with the thought that she would blame me for you and Cynthia not getting back together. There would always be that tension hanging over our heads." She was sobbing. "What we had was special, Romel, but it doesn't look like it's going to work out."

He wrapped his arms around her, tears stinging his eyes. "Please."

She wriggled from him and sat on the bottom step of the staircase.

He kneeled in front of her. "Princess isn't here. Can't we just have supper? I can't stand the thought of eating supper without you."

"Are you asking me to resume a relationship—"

"I'm asking for us to spend evenings together. Figure out how to get back to where we were before our kids came home."

She stared at him, her red face puffy and her eyes filled with doubt. "What you're asking me to do is continue a relationship based on your daughter's whims. I just can't go through that."

Romel stood and scraped his fingers across his scalp. "You're right. It's not fair of me. I'll just get Bert and leave you be."

This was ridiculous. Princess had been back in Los Angeles for over two weeks and still refused to change her mind. Why couldn't she be more like Tommy and give Georgia a chance? If Tommy and Dana hadn't gone to Peru on a buying trip for Dana's shop, Romel would have relied on Tommy to help convince Princess that Georgia wasn't the enemy. As it was, Romel had to count on Cynthia to help Princess understand what Georgia meant to him.

"Hi, Daddy. Did you call to check on Mama? She's not here."

"I called to ask if she talked to you." He raked his hands through his hair, squeezed the back of his neck.

"Yeah." Her tone was dismissive. "She told me you two talked."

"Good. So, you understand we both want to move on, right?"

"I don't believe it, Daddy." Her voice trembled. "Mama is lonely and you're being mean."

"Please don't cry, Princess." His mouth fell open, and he rubbed his week-old whiskers. "I'm not trying to be mean. Your mama wants me to be happy with Georgia. I wish you did too."

"I'll never like her! And I'll never forgive you if you marry someone else. Mama will change her mind." The click of the phone line punctured his already damaged heart.

Romel snapped his phone shut and loaded his truck. He'd finish painting the last wall of the shelter. And if he ran into Georgia, he'd be friendly, but not push her. He refused to give up on their relationship—he figured Georgia needed time the same as Princess.

At the shelter, he looked for Georgia's car and swore his ribs tightened around his lungs when her car wasn't there. Inhaling was difficult, and he probably should have forced himself to eat something, but the heat, coupled with his lack of interest, won out. Romel mopped sweat from his brow, took a sip of water, and hefted the heavier than usual five-gallon bucket of paint to the manlift. The engine shuddered as the cage ascended to the second story, then sputtered to a stop. The last time Romel had trouble with the engine, he'd forgotten his cell phone in the truck and been forced to shimmy down the boom. He patted the cell in his shirt pocket. At least he could call for help if he absolutely had to, but he also knew he stood the best chance of getting the engine started if he let it sit. And he likely had only one chance for the engine to turn over. He didn't really want to call for help. Didn't want to bother anyone with rescuing him.

Another delay. At this rate, he'd have difficulty meeting his deadline. He may not be able to handle his relationships with women, but he prided himself on handling deadlines in his business.

He licked his dry lips and surveyed his project. He'd spray what he could from his current position and then deal with the engine.

Romel pried the lid from the bucket of paint. When he lifted the bucket, his head reeled, and he stumbled a bit, knocking his water bottle over the edge. He peered over the scaffold. Thank goodness he'd remembered to put up his safety cones around the perimeter, and no one was in the play yard yet this afternoon.

Midday rays from the sun ricocheted off the metal cage, searing his face with bright light. Within ten minutes, he'd be done painting what he could reach, then he'd deal with the engine and go cool off in the break room. His mouth was already parched, but another twenty minutes without water wasn't going to kill him.

Minutes later, muscle cramps seized his calves, and he was lightheaded. He peered at the controls. Which one started the engine? Blue or red?

Romel pressed the blue. Laid his forehead on the panel. Coughs and sputters filled the oppressive air. Salty sweat stung his eyes, and saliva refused to form. He had to get down.

He pressed again. The engine gasped and rumbled but didn't die. What next? Unhook the tether. Push the joystick. Step on the foot pedal. The boom jerked upward. Romel's hands flew from the controls and knocked off his sunglasses. The sun pierced his eyes, and he stumbled backward until his back slammed into the metal bars of the cage. Engine fumes assaulted him; he fell to his knees and vomited—the stench adding to his inability to reason. He looked around. The boom was still in the air. He needed help, but no words would form.

Focus. Pull yourself up. Pull the lever. Hit the foot pedal.

Unable to stand upright, Romel collapsed over the panel, the boom moving downward. The ground rose up to meet him, and the cage shuddered to a stop. He stepped toward the sound of her voice.

Georgia.

Georgia crossed the shelter parking lot, her gaze drawn to the manlift. Romel was draped over the control panel. Georgia tugged at the hem of her shirt and glared at him. Her gut turned inside out. Romel should be standing. Why wasn't he?

The basket descended but stopped a foot above the pavement. She ran toward him. Called his name. He half stood, angled his head toward her, and opened the gate. Her feet were swift, but his head hit the pavement before she reached him.

Dropping to her knees, she checked his pulse. Almost imperceptible. Don't move him. Dial 9-1-1. Talk to him. Reassure him. Hold his hand.

"Please, God. Don't take him from me."

Georgia pressed her cheek to Romel's. Whispered she was there. Told him she loved him. Lights flashed and a siren sounded. Paramedics slapped an oxygen mask over his mouth and took his vitals. "Are you his wife?"

"No, I'm"—she buried her face in her hands—"I'm a friend."

"Any idea which hospital he prefers?"

"No. Take him to Hilo Community."

She followed the gurney and stepped into the ambulance. "Ma'am? You can't ride back here."

"I'm a nurse. I'm not leaving."

He smacked his lips. "You can ride in the cab. Does he have any family?"

"He has kids."

"Do you know how to reach them?"

"Their numbers are in his cell phone." The paramedic checked Romel's pockets and handed her the phone.

"You might want to call them."

Georgia held his phone in her hand, squeezed her eyes closed, and shook her head. The paramedic's firm voice demanded her attention. "Look, lady, you need to move to the cab so we can get him to the hospital."

She opened her eyes, blinked, and saw Lani standing behind the ambulance. Georgia kissed Romel's forehead and stepped out of the ambulance. She fell into Lani's open arms. "Will you drive me to the hospital?"

Lani ushered her to the car. "I heard the siren. What happened?"

"He fell and hit his head." Georgia covered her face with her hands. "He barely has a pulse."

"It's a good thing you were there when it happened."

The vision of his head hitting the pavement made her stomach roil. "Pull over. I'm going to be sick."

Lani had barely stopped the car before Georgia threw the door open and retched onto the pavement. She wiped her mouth with a tissue and drank a sip of water from the bottle Lani offered her. "I can't lose him."

"I know, sweetie. I know." Lani rubbed her back. "Are you ready to go?"

"I think so." Georgia took several ragged breaths. Had Romel heard her admit she still loved him? What if the last thing he remembered her saying was that she wouldn't wait for him to work things out with Princess?

Lani dropped Georgia at the emergency room entrance. "You go in. I'll find you."

Fluorescent lights and the smell of antiseptic assaulted Georgia's senses. She rushed to the desk and asked where they'd taken Romel and was told he was down the hall, and she should sit in the waiting area. Unable to touch the orange vinyl chairs she'd sat in the day William died, she leaned against the wall. Lightheaded and heartsick, she fought the persistent doom that threatened to consume her. The calls to Tommy and Princess would wait until she had more information. She bit her lips, massaged her temples, and reminded herself to be strong for Romel.

The *thrum, thrum, thrumming* of a gurney coming down the hall sent her scrambling. It was Romel—a cervical collar supported his neck, and an oxygen mask covered his mouth. His eyes were closed.

Georgia approached the entourage. "How is he?"

"Are you family?" A doctor asked.

"No. I'm a friend."

"Were you with him when he fell?"

"Yes. I mean, I saw him fall."

"Then I'd like to ask you some questions."

"But will he be okay?"

"That's what we're trying to figure out."

They rolled Romel's unresponsive body into the elevator. Georgia wrung her hands. "Where are they taking him?"

"That's confidential information. Follow me, please." The doctor led Georgia to an empty room. "Please sit. I'm Dr. Igawa."

Georgia sat on the edge of the fabric chair, squeezed her hands together in her lap, and answered a barrage of questions as best she could. She didn't know many of the answers except who his kids were. She didn't know what he'd eaten that day, whether he had any drug allergies, or what health directives were in place. Dr. Igawa didn't ask the questions she knew the answers to—was he kind? Considerate? Gentle? Tears dampened her cheeks.

"Ms. Weber?"

Georgia startled and wiped her face with the back of her hand. Dr. Igawa softened his tone. "I was asking what Mr. Bautista was doing right before he fell? We're trying to figure out what triggered the fall."

"He was painting. He's a painter."

"What kind of painting?"

"Buildings. He was painting the exterior of the animal shelter."

"Anything else you can tell me?"

Georgia twisted her fingers together. "He had a headache and nausea a couple of weeks ago. Said he just needed to hydrate and cool down."

"Do you know if that's normal for him?"

Her shoulders shook, and her chin quivered. "I don't know what's normal."

Dr. Igawa stood. "The EMT said he advised you to call his children."

She nodded and willed her chin to stop trembling.

"Were you able to reach them?"

"I haven't tried yet. I thought I should have something to tell them about their dad's condition first."

Dr. Igawa rubbed his chin. "That's a problem, because I can't legally share that information with you."

"I'm a nurse. I'm familiar with HIPAA."

"Then you understand my limitations with sharing medical information."

"I recommend you contact his next of kin and have them call me as soon as possible." He scribbled a number on a piece of scratch paper and handed it to her. "I need next of kin to make the decisions on the treatment plan."

Did that mean Romel was dying? "I'll try, but the eldest is in Peru."

"Is the other child at least eighteen?"

"She's eighteen but she's ... she's immature."

"Look, Ms. Weber, the law says if she's eighteen she can make the decisions." He stood and patted her shoulder. "I assure you I'll give her all the information she needs to make an informed decision."

Chapter Thirteen

GEORGIA'S FEET WERE ROOTED to the white tile floor of the broad hallway, her gaze fixed on the elevator, and her thoughts a jumbled mess.

"Sweetie?" Lani's voice drifted in from the abyss. "Let's sit."

Georgia shook her head. "I can't."

"Okay." Lani wrapped her arm around Georgia's waist. "That's okay. We can stand."

"He's still unconscious. I don't know where they've taken him."

"Then we'll wait. Did you call his kids?"

"Not yet." Georgia's addled brain was incapable of wrapping her head around the thought that Princess might be in charge of making the medical decisions for Romel. God help him. "The doctor said to call. He wants to talk to one of them on the phone so they can decide on a treatment plan. What if I can't reach Tommy? How can Princess make a medical decision?" Georgia blinked rapidly, heat flushed her cheeks.

"Call Tommy first. I'll be right here if you need me."

Georgia's gaze darted around the lobby. There were a few others sitting in the orange chairs now. She wanted to stay near the elevator in case they brought Romel back down, and she wanted some privacy. She walked to the quietest corner of the small room and pulled up Tommy's number on Romel's cell phone.

No answer. What should she say in a voice message? She steadied her voice. "This is Georgia, your dad's friend. Call back as soon as you can."

Bile stung her throat. Princess had to be informed. Georgia fumbled with Romel's phone. Pressed Princess on favorite contacts.

"Hi, Daddy. Did you change your mind about Mama?"

Georgia gulped down the scream rising in her chest. "Princess, it's Georgia."

"Why are you on Daddy's phone?" An accusation.

"Your dad had an accident." Georgia pressed the phone to her ear and whispered the words, "he's in the hospital."

"But he'll be okay, right?"

"It's too soon to know. They can't tell me what's going on. His doctor wants you to call him."

"Me? What about Mama? Or Tommy?"

"I left a voice message for Tommy, and the doctor can't share information with your mom. I'll text Dr. Igawa's number." Georgia steadied her breath. "And Princess, you need to come as soon as possible."

Princess's screams slammed into Georgia's eardrum. She pressed the phone to her ear; absorbed the animal sound so the others in the waiting area wouldn't hear. Georgia's heart splintered into a million pieces.

"I ... I don't ... have enough money. And Mama doesn't either."

"I'll buy you a ticket. Your dad would want you here."

"Okay." The sound of a frightened little girl, not a sassy teenager. "What about Tommy?"

"I left him a message to call me. Text me your legal name and birth date and head for the airport. I'll send you the travel information as soon as I can."

Georgia's heart pounded in her ears. The poor kid.

Less than an hour later, the flights were secured. Princess called. "I'm at the airport and the nurse can't find the doctor to talk to me. Can't you find out what's going on?"

"I wish I could. Since I'm not family, they can't tell me, but I'm sure your dad is getting the best care possible. Try not to worry. My friend Lani will pick you up when you get to Hilo. I'll see you later tonight."

"Okay."

"You said all the right things." Lani nudged her elbow. "You're doing great. How about some lunch?"

"I'm not hungry."

"Coffee?"

"Not right now." Georgia glanced at her watch. "Would you mind going to the house and checking on Onyx?"

"Sure." Lani took the house keys from Georgia, gave her a hug, and said she'd be back in an hour or so.

Romel's phone rang. "Georgia? It's Tommy. What's going on?"

She relayed what she knew about Romel's accident and told him Princess was on her way.

"We're in Peru. I don't know how quickly we can get back."

Georgia's throat seized. "The doctor wants to talk to you. I'll text the number. Would you let me know what he says? They can't tell me anything."

"I'll do that."

"Will you ...will you tell dad I love him?"

She chewed the inside of her cheek. "I will."

Waiting for Tommy to call back was excruciating. Not knowing what was wrong with Romel was even more excruciating.

Finally, Romel's phone buzzed in her hands. Georgia pressed the phone to her ear. Tommy relayed the information. "It looks like a concussion." His voice dropped to a near whisper. "They don't know how bad until they do an MRI."

Georgia steadied herself for Tommy's sake. "Then we'll need to wait for the results."

"I asked Dr. Igawa to let you sit with Dad. I don't want him alone if ... when he wakes up."

"Thank you. I'm grateful."

"I'm glad you're there. I'll keep my phone handy."

She'd get to see Romel. Let him know Princess was on her way and that they all loved him.

The ICU charge nurse checked Georgia's ID against the list of approved visitors, then escorted her to Romel's bed.

Georgia recognized the signs of distress—knew them well from her days in the emergency room—the tightened brow, the flailing head, the heart-wrenching moaning. The eerie green lights of the heart monitor that recorded his erratic heart rate.

Her stomach coiled and bile rose in the back of her throat, but she stroked Romel's forearm and talked to him in a voice as calm as she could muster.

She reached in her pocket, pulled out her keychain, and stared at the word engraved on it. Believe. She had to stay positive. Had to believe Romel would get better. Georgia texted an update to Lani. Lani responded she was at the airport to pick up Princess, and they would be at the hospital soon.

Georgia knew Princess had arrived by the audible gasp from the doorway. Georgia watched helplessly as Princess ran to her dad and collapsed across his chest, sobbing.

One of the ICU nurses scrambled to Romel's bedside and escorted Princess out of the room. Georgia followed and heard the nurse explain to Princess that she had to maintain her composure, or they'd insist she leave. Georgia approached the nurse and assured her Princess would be okay.

Georgia walked down the hallway and spoke to Princess in a soothing voice. "Talk to him. He can probably hear you. That's why we need to stay calm. He needs to know he'll be okay."

"What do I say?"

"Tell him how much you love him. The doctor thinks he can hear us. Hold his hand. He needs reassurance."

Princess pulled herself together before she reentered the room. Georgia dabbed at tears when Princess told her dad how Georgia had bought her a ticket so she could come see him, and added, "Wasn't that nice of her?"

Romel shifted and his eyelids blinked rapidly. "What's happening?"

Princess grabbed Georgia's hand.

"Get the nurse," Georgia commanded. Please, God, don't let it be a seizure.

Georgia and Princess stood back while the nurse checked Romel's pupils and spoke to him. Georgia glared at the monitors. Princess buried her head in her hands and Georgia pulled her into a motherly hug.

The nurse instructed Romel to squeeze her finger if he could hear her. Georgia stared at his hand. Her breath caught as she watched his fingers form a loose fist around the nurse's finger. "Welcome back, Mr. Bautista. Don't try to talk yet."

"Hi, Daddy." Princess took his hand, and Georgia stood behind her.

The nurse dabbed his lips and tongue with an oral swab. "It's okay to talk now."

He uttered, "What the hell happened?"

"Oh, Daddy." Princess kissed his cheek. "You hit your head. You're okay now."

Romel's eyes darted from Georgia to Princess to the monitors. "Georgia?"

She moved to his bedside and touched his cheek with her hand. "Don't ever scare us like that again, okay?"

"Okay."

Two days later, the doctor stood at the edge of Romel's bed. "You were severely dehydrated when you arrived. That's probably what caused you to pass out. Unfortunately, your head hit pavement, and *fortunately*, Ms. Weber called the ambulance right away."

Romel smiled up at Georgia. The doctor continued, "We'll keep you for observation to make sure your organs weren't affected."

"When can I get out of here?"

"As soon as you're able to walk without feeling dizzy. A couple of days, probably. I'll check in tomorrow."

Romel turned to Georgia. "I can't wait to get out of here."

She kissed his cheek. "I talked to Tommy this morning and convinced them to finish their trip to Machu Picchu. I think he'd feel a whole lot better if he could talk to you."

"Get him on the line for me, will you? I don't need my kids missing out on things because of me."

Romel talked with Tommy and assured him he was doing fine.

Princess walked into the room, said hello to Georgia, and gave Romel a hug. "I talked to Mom this morning. She sends her love."

Romel squeezed Georgia's hand.

"Did you talk to your teachers about all the class time you're missing?"

"About that..."

Romel pursed his lips. "I'm fine, Princess. You should get back to school."

"I don't want to go back."

"What's your plan then?"

"I don't have a plan. I thought I'd just hang out with you for the rest of the summer and then see what happens. Maybe I can get a job at the frozen yogurt place or something."

"If you want to move back home, that's fine, but not just because I got hurt." Romel shook his head. "You'll have to get a job."

"I will, Daddy. After you're better." She looked at Georgia. "I can take care of you by myself."

Romel looked at Georgia. Her face was pinched, hurt in her eyes. But he couldn't ask her to take care of him, even though she was a nurse, when he wasn't sure where they stood. Maybe with more time with Princess, he could convince her to accept Georgia. That is, if Georgia had changed her mind about giving him time to work things out with his daughter. They hadn't talked about what came next.

Chapter Fourteen

Georgia called Romel the day after he got out of the hospital. Princess answered and informed her that Romel was done with her. That Cynthia was flying home soon, so she could take care of him. That her parents were getting back together.

That was that, then. How easily Romel slipped into staying away from her now that Princess was home. How easily he fell back into Cynthia's arms. But she'd like to hear it from Romel's mouth. Make him look her in the eye and tell her he didn't love her. Admit to her that he never stopped loving Cynthia.

She'd take a supper dish. Confront him. Talk to him before Cynthia arrived. Remind him he and Cynthia had divorced for a reason.

She'd tell him she loved him, and she'd fight for him. He'd have to choose. Then, she'd kiss him, so he'd remember what they once had together.

The Crockpot was heavy in her hands as she carried it to Romel's front door. She leaned her elbow against the doorbell, rehearsing what to say and what not to say.

The door flung open. "Oh, it's you." Princess screwed up her mouth and pushed the door nearly closed. "I thought our pizza was here."

"I brought you some supper." Georgia pasted on a smile. "You can keep it for another meal."

Georgia thrust the Crockpot forward, but Princess made no effort to take it. "How's Romel?"

"We're doing just fine."

"May I take this to the kitchen for you?"

Princess looked beyond Georgia. The pizza delivery gal bounded up to the lanai.

"Who's that at the door?" Romel's voice cut through the confusion.

"Our pizza's here," Princess shouted back, still guarding the door like a sentry.

Georgia stepped backward. Why wouldn't Princess tell Romel she was at the door? "Romel? It's Georgia. May I come in?"

"He doesn't want to see you. I told you that."

"Georgia. I've been wanting to talk to you." Romel opened the door wider, stood behind his daughter. "Princess, take the pizza to the kitchen."

She grabbed the pizza and huffed away. The delivery gal shrugged and scurried to her van. "Here." Romel reached for the Crockpot. "Let me take that. Come in."

Georgia followed him into the house. He set the pot on the dining room table. His shoulders were up around his ears. "I don't know what's been going on, but I aim to find out."

"Wait." Georgia touched his arm. "Could we talk first? I have something to say, and I don't want to lose my nerve."

He cocked his head. Georgia licked her lips. "I still love you and if you think you and Cynthia can make it together, think about why you didn't make it the first time. Why you came running after me when she came to town."

She kept her gaze on him. He opened his mouth to speak, and she covered his lips with her fingertips. "*Shh*. Don't say anything until I'm done."

This was her last defense. He could send her away, but at least she would have tried to help him remember what they had. "Kiss me."

His arms wrapped around her, and his lips pressed into hers. There was a new urgency to the kiss and a renewal of a life together. He grinned when he finished and held her chin in his palm. "I miss you. I miss *us*. I don't know why you're still talking about Cynthia."

"Because Princess called and informed me that you did not want to talk to me anymore. That Cynthia was coming home so you could get back together."

"She what?" Romel scraped his hand over his scalp. "She told me *you* called when I was resting my first day home. That you wanted me to leave you be so you could move on with your life. It sounded like something you might say."

"She really does dislike me." Georgia lowered her chin. "Are you going to allow her to dictate your life, Romel?"

"No." He took Georgia's hand and pulled her to the kitchen.

Princess sat at the table, eating pizza, and playing on her phone. "Daddy?"

"Put down the phone, young lady. We need to have a talk."

Her eyes widened, and she looked from Georgia to her dad. "You sound mad. What did Georgia tell you?"

Romel told her they knew what she'd done.

Tears gathered. "I just want our family together."

Georgia's hand tightened around Romel's. "It's time you accept it—your mama and I will never get back together. I love Georgia."

Princess looked at Georgia. "I don't hate you."

"I know this is difficult," Georgia said. "And you don't have to like me. But I'm going to keep coming around because I love your dad."

"I love him too."

"And I love you both," Romel said. "And somehow, we are going to figure this out together, okay?"

Princess bit her lip. "Okay, Daddy."

Romel was glad Georgia offered to give Princess a couple of weeks to sort out her feelings before they tried to do something together, just the three of them. Every day, he thought about Georgia, but only talked to her on the phone. In the meantime, while he was still waiting for his doctor to give him a release to go back to work, he fretted about falling behind on his painting contracts.

Romel hung up his phone and sighed. "That was the last client. Good people. They all understood I need more time to complete my contracts on painting their houses."

"I'm glad, Daddy. I know it bothers you, just like it bothers you that I messed up. I'm sorry I caused problems between you and Georgia."

"I forgive you, Princess."

"If you love her, why aren't you seeing her?"

"We thought you might need some time to get used to the idea. I'd love to go see her. And I'd love it more if we could invite her to come play Monopoly with us."

Princess set up straight. "We could invite her to dinner and then play."

"I'd like that. I'll call and invite her."

"Let me call. That way, she'll know I don't mind."

Chapter Fifteen

Georgia paused at Romel's front door and smoothed down her hair. Princess's invitation to come for supper and game night had caught Georgia off guard since it was only a few days after she and Romel had confronted Princess. Hopefully, the girl was sincere.

Romel opened the door before she could knock and pulled her into his arms. "I missed you. Kiss me."

"I missed you too." She glanced around before settling her mouth on his. "Where's Princess?"

"In the kitchen fussing over which plates to use"—his grin faded, and his expression turned serious—"I swear she's ready to accept us. She's even talked about going back to Los Angeles. Her teachers at the beauty school will allow her to make up the weeks she missed."

Princess's voice sounded from the kitchen. "Daddy, where are the sterling salad tongs? I want everything to be perfect for Georgia."

Georgia's shoulders relaxed. She looked heavenward.

After supper, Georgia helped Romel load the dishwasher while Princess set up the Monopoly game. She'd been quite talkative during their meal with no sign of whining or complaint. Now she screwed up her mouth and stared at the game tokens she held in her hand.

"Ready?" Romel asked.

Princess held out her token-filled palm to Georgia. "You choose first."

There was no question. Georgia picked out the little Scottie dog. Princess opened her mouth. Closed it. Looked at Romel and sucked in a breath. "Good choice."

Georgia would have to ask Romel later what that look was about, especially since the exchange ended with Romel beaming and squeezing his daughter's hand. Or maybe it wasn't important. The evening was a success. For now, that was all that mattered.

Back at home and feeling quite contented, Georgia reached down and ran her fingers through Onyx's coat, then roamed back to the den and the aviary. She spied one of Bert's feathers and bent to pick it up. What a waste to have this beautiful aviary and not one bird to enjoy it.

The next morning Georgia drove to the animal shelter and looked in on the Dobies. She cuddled the runt of the litter and wondered whether Onyx would get along with an active pup. She carried the little one to Lani's office and announced she'd like to adopt her and take Trudy back home.

Lani smiled. "What does Romel think about sharing you with all these critters?"

"I'm going to surprise him."

Georgia played with her pets the rest of the day. She took Onyx to the backyard and threw the ball for him while the Dobie pup wove in and out of Onyx's legs, nipping at him and yelping for attention. Trudy paced her new perch, flew around the house, and squawked. It was chaotic and noisy, and Georgia loved every uproarious minute of it.

She was no longer afraid of taking care of these living things. After she'd fed all the animals and settled into her evening, she decided not to vacuum the floors or do her supper dishes. That could wait. Right now, she just wanted to watch her pup nuzzle into Onyx's chest and enjoy Onyx's feigned annoyance. And what better sound than listening to Trudy chant, "Pretty bird."

At the sound of the doorbell, Onyx jumped up and barked, and the little Dobie followed suit. Trudy squawked and flapped her wings. Who would be visiting at this hour?

Georgia opened the door. Romel stood on her lanai, a pie carrier in one hand, and a look of anticipation written across his face. "I hope it's okay to come unannounced. I had to see you, pretty lady."

She set the pie carrier aside and melted into his arms.

"I feel so empty when we're apart." Romel tilted her chin and brushed his lips across hers. "I don't want to wait any longer. I don't have a ring, but say you'll marry me."

She looked around at her pets. "We come as a set. Will you have me and all my marvelous animals?"

Romel threw his head back and laughed. "It's a deal."

Jacquolyn McMurray is published in both contemporary and historical romance. She and her husband live on a Christmas tree farm on the island of Hawai'i where they feed a clowder of cats and a flock of hodgepodge chickens.

She can be contacted at:
jacquolyn@jacquolynmcmurray.com

Mele Kalikimaka Sweet Hawaiian Romance

Always on Christmas

Christmas at the Aloha Cafe

Wanted: A Groom for Christmas

Historical Romance

Woven Hearts